A Perfect Face for Radio

James K. Flynn

Foreword by Robert Inman   Backword by Doug Robarchek

Copyright © 2008 by James K. Flynn

A Perfect Face for Radio

All rights reserved. No part of this book may be reproduced or transmitted in any form or by any means, electronic, or mechanical, including photocopying, recording or by any information storage and retrieval system, without permission in writing from the publisher. No abridgement or changes to the text are authorized by the publisher.

ISBN number: 978-1-59712-287-0

Printed in the United States of America by
Catawba Publishing Company

Order from:
Catawba Publishing Company
(704) 717-8452
www.catawbapublishing.com

For Donna,

who always gets

the first edit...

Contents

Introduction & Acknowledgements   i
Foreward   iii

Funny

All I Need to Know About AT&T I Learned in Kindergarten	1
What? No Post-Apocalypse Skills?	5
The Evening News	7
Let's Make A Deal	9
CEO Compensation Taxes My Math Skills	11
Charlotte Traffic? Try Chicago	13
Defending My Right Not to Bare Chins	15
Even a Lawsuit Tastes Better When It Sits on a Ritz	17
Dear Santa@northpole.com	19
Credit Where Credit is Due	21
Alex Forever	23
Business Humor	25
Science Quiz 2000	27
Did You File Your Form 10-Pharaoh?	29
Pixie Dust at the Bargaining Table	33
SouthPark – TV or Not TV?	35
A Dollar By Any Other Name	39
TV Sweeps Appeal to Greed	41
Hornets Insider? Not Exactly	43
Science 101 Quiz	45
"Reykjavik, We Have a Problem . . ."	47
The Russians and Ronald McDonald	49
The Envelope, Please	51
Letter to Santa v.1999	53
In a New York Minute	55
I Love a Parade	57
Predictions for the New Year 2001	59
Peanut Airlines	61
Does Your Sign Have a Cork In It?	65
License Plate, Thy Name is Vanity	67
The Web's Ten Worst Sites	69
One Less Pole Sign	71
Starquakes!	73

Funny? Not so much...	75
Goodbye, Checkie	77
An American Hero . . . Who Fixes Trucks	79
Ad of Infamy	81
Oh, Say . . . Can You Sing?	83
Radio - Where is the Public Service?	85
Memo to a Sports Critic	87
"Ol' Hugo Was a'Messin'..."	89
Charlotte: A City That's a Cut Above the Rest	93
What Should a Southerner Salute?	95
Broadcasting's Life Blood	97
City Council Reality Shows? Why Not?	99
Turn Me Loose on Traffic Scofflaws	101
Crossing the Comedy Line	103
So, What's an Old Bus Station to You?	105
Inside a Re-zoning Battle	107
Oprah's Web	109
Primaries, Deaths and DMV	111
Let's Skip the Flag Fashions	113
What Color's My Grassroots?	115
Support Live Theater	117
Bumps in the Election Road	119
My Tenure as Community Columnist	121
Backword	123

Introduction & Acknowledgements

"I'm in favor of keeping dangerous weapons out of the hands of fools. Let's start with typewriters."

- Solomon Short -

Ah, the audacity of the writer. To be so egotistical to think you're good enough to string a few nouns and verbs together, sprinkle in a soupcon of adjectives and dare to place the dreaded semicolon where you just *know* it's used correctly and then believe it's worth someone's time and effort to read and appreciate said string… audacity.

And yet, in this Age of the Blog, audacity reigns supreme. Anyone with access to the Internet feels almost obligated to foist their thoughts on a public that seems hungry for more and more words, no matter the topic, slant, grammar - or lack thereof.

The difference lies in that those of us who aim for being published in the "legitimate" press still have to go through a journalistic gauntlet. Yes, there still remains one person who can nip audacity in the bud: the editor. "Writers' ego" is to "editor" as "balloon" is to "hot pin."

But even as the op-ed writer's ego sits whimpering in a corner after years of the editorial carrot-and-stick, it is not cowed enough to keep it from collating it's work and audaciously publishing it as a *book*, hoping against hope that, if readers liked it the first time, they'll pay to read it *again*.

In case this is your first venture into my little op-ed world, these columns appeared in The Charlotte Observer and The Business Journal. The Journal columns were published under the byline "Point Askew" and were intended to be humorous. (They won a North Carolina Press Association award for Humor Columns so somebody must've laughed.) The Observer pieces were more in the standard op-ed milieu, with a dozen written during my stint as a

Community Columnist. And there's a few that never saw the, um, ink of day and were wandering waif-like around my hard drive saying, "Please sir, may I have some print?"… so I tossed 'em in.

My thanks to Jane McAlister Pope and Joanne Skoog, my editors at the Observer and Journal, respectively.

Thanks to Robert Inman and Doug Robarchek. Bob's a *real* writer and a friend. Doug may be one of the funniest writers around and I promised if he wrote the Backward I'd buy a copy of *his* book.

The cover caricature was drawn by the talented Jerry Frazee and colorized by the equally talented Ian Flynn. My thanks to them.

And thank you for buying this book. (If you're someone that I gave a copy to, consider it your duty to be Amway-like in your promotion of it.)

JKF
August, 2008

Foreward

by Robert Inman

Okay, so you're in Hawaii on vacation, relaxing in your room at the Waikiki Mega-Hotel after a strenuous hula skirt competition. You turn on the TV and there's a commercial for Outback Steakhouse. And this voice. You've heard it somewhere before, and it's driving you nuts that you can't think of where. And then you think: *it's the same guy who used to warn me over the loudspeaker at the Charlotte airport not to leave my bag where terrorists can get it.* And then you remember that voice on your car radio a few years ago, soothing your jangled nerves as you navigated I-77. Same guy. A voice so distinctive you'll remember it fifty years from now. The voice of your favorite uncle, telling you that even though the planet's falling apart, it's all right because there are still a lot of good people inhabiting the place, and NASCAR is alive and well.

Okay, you've nailed the voice, and then you put it with a body, a face. Saw this guy in a stage play – maybe Theatre Charlotte or Children's Theatre. You rummage through the stack of playbills clogging your nightstand drawer and there it is: James K. Flynn.

Can you believe this guy? Radio personality, actor, voice talent, uncle to millions. And now, writer.

Surprised? I'm sure not. I've known James K. for…well, let's not date ourselves. A lot of years. Anybody who communicates the way he does is bound to write well. After all, stringing words and sentences together is the best way we have of organizing our thoughts, ideas, memories, myths and legends.

The best kind of writing is storytelling. Tell me a fact and I may or may not remember it. Tell me a story that illustrates the fact, and it sticks. From the abstract to the concrete.

All stories are about people – some real, some made-up. The best stories are about people we recognize, whether they're real or fictional. They're us, or at least enough like us to be believable and intriguing. We take a leap of faith into their story and let them entertain, inform, educate, even disturb us.

What you have here in this book is what my Uncle Ed used to call a bunch of "dang good yarns." They're stories about people you won't soon forget, and yes, you'll find some of yourself in them. James K. has a wonderful gift for plucking nuggets from the everyday mundane and fashioning them into captivating and memorable stories. When you've finished this book, you will feel like you know these people, and you'll know James K. There are lots of nuggets here. And gems.

Oh, and one other thing I like about James K: he and I agree that Doug Robarchek is one of the funniest men on the planet, and should probably be committed.

Funny

All I Need to Know About AT&T I Learned in Kindergarten

Originally published July 27, 1998
© Charlotte Business Journal. All rights reserved.
Reprinted with permission

The scene: 1 p.m. at the new Financial Immersion Kindergarten.

All right, class. Since you've been very good today, we've decided you can have a story before nap time. Look who's here! It's Mr. Media!

Yaaay!

Hi, boys and girls. What do you want?

Tell us a good story, please, Mr. Media?

OK, boys and girls. Lie down on your futons and make sure the lids on your lattes are on reeeal tight . . .

Once upon a time there was a very famous lady named Old Ma Bell. One day, people noticed Ma Bell had gotten real big. Everybody said it was a bunch of Baby Bells, but nobody could figure out who Daddy Bell was, so there was a scandal. Can you say "scandal" boys and girls?

Monica!

No, this was long before that.

Ollie?

No, even before that.

Watergate?

Give it a rest, kids.

OK, Mr. Media.

Because of the scandal, her mean ol' Uncle Sam told Ma Bell she had to give away all the Baby Bells.

Awww, that's sad!

Well, kind of. But they all went to good homes across the country and grew up to be Big Baby Bells.

Yaay!

The Baby Bells even talked to Ma Bell. Sometimes. They weren't always nice. The Baby Bells would say bad things about ol' Ma and take money away from her. Ma Bell couldn't even spank them anymore, because they got to be so big.

Bad Big Baby Bells!

Nice alliteration, boys and girls. Now, ol' Ma Bell, even though she was being dissed big time by her children, was still a tough ol' mama. She was still invited to all the fancy parties. She traveled around the world. She surfed the Net. And do you know what she found?

Daddy Bell?

Close. She found a new boyfriend.

Who was it?

Mr. Eye.

CBS?

No, Mr. T.C. Eye. He's the man who brings cable TV to millions of boys and girls.

Yaay!

Ma Bell and T.C. were very happy together. Ma gave T.C. a great big dowry so they could get married. Can you say "dowry" and "married" boys and girls?

Stock swap and cash! Merger!

Very good! And faster than a Teletubbie can kick a Power Ranger off a toy shelf, ol' Ma Bell was back to take on those Baby Bells again.

Did they live happily ever after?

Mr. Media doesn't know, boys and girls. Some of Mr. Media's hired experts think Ma Bell's dowry was too big. But you can bet Mr. Media will be watching this marriage very closely. Almost as close as the Baby Bells. So, what did we learn from this story?

Always be nice to your Ma!

Yes! Anything else?

Deregulate and let the market sort it out!

Very good. 'Bye, boys and girls!

'Bye, Mr. Media!

Now, go right to sleep. When you get up it'll be scissors and glue time and we'll make nice collages out of back issues of Forbes.

Yaay!

What? No Post-Apocalypse Skills?

Originally published August 24, 1998
© Charlotte Business Journal. All rights reserved.
Reprinted with permission

Welcome to my nightmare.

Each of us has a situation that we dread we'll be a part of - a giant earthquake, walking into a really big web full of hairy spiders, having the second phrase of your column end in a preposition – pretty terrifying stuff. I want to let you in on mine. I want to TESTIFY!

I play solitaire on the computer. Yeah, like, you don't? Why do you think the government's after Bill Gates? A monopoly? Oh, please. The real reason is some CEO's special assistant burnt up the mouse chasing that red seven. Because the sales department wanted to win one more game of FreeCell before they started their obligatory cold calls. Because there are thousands of offices out there in Business Land that grind to a halt on a regular basis when the action of the Microsoft Hearts Network is *hot*. But I digress . . .

I play when I should be working. Just the other night, when Daddy was "upstairs writing," my nine year old son caught me in the middle of a tenacious game of Vegas Solitaire. The PC gods were smiling. I capped off the last king. The cards wheeled in their little Pentium mambo, ending in a bright green screen asking if I wanted to "Deal Again?"

My son said, "Gee, Dad. You're good!"

There was no pretense. He actually thought his dad was King of the Keyboard. Master of the Mouse. Sultan of Solitaire. He was proud of me.

There's something heady that comes from the unabashed adoration of a child. It is a fleeting feeling. I know, deep down in my primordial core, that sooner or later he'll grow up, work a computer with the same ease I manage trimming my toenails and leave me in my old age, wheezing in his binary dust. But right now, he's proud.

But was his pride based on the two novels I have lurking on the hard drive? The three dozen short stories searching for a publisher? The wall full of advertising awards? Nope. I play no-prisoners solitaire. It gave me pause. And brought me to my nightmare.

It's after World War Three on Earth. India has obliterated Pakistan. China, defending its borders, has taken out India and, oops - ha-ha, one little rascally Scud slipped into Taiwan. America and Russia heave a couple of MIRV's at China and France launches at the United States because it's a good excuse to get back at us for introducing *Le Drugstore* into their language.

The radiation. Nuclear winter. Those are the up-sides, along with the fact all the talk-show hosts will be vaporized in the first strike. No, the *bad* thing is I survived.

And have no marketable skills whatsoever.

After they drop the Big One, what is going to be in demand? Society will need professionals to help it get back on its feet. Doctors, mechanical and electrical engineers, even farmers that can get the crops perked up will be the new barons of Armageddon Industry. And I'll be at the bottom of the post-apocalyptic pecking order, right there with politicians, radio sales people and the Spice Girls.

Think about it. The last vestiges of humanity are scrapping for survival and the best I've got to offer is a dynamite Mr. Haney impression and my prowess at Solitaire. I'm a damn good public address announcer, but with the NBA experiencing a 30 megaton lockout, there goes *that* gig. If I only had something to offer my fellow survivors, a mastery of some necessary craft...

<u>Bloodied, but bold Leader</u> – "This computer is our last hope to get the power back on so the old people and children won't freeze. Suggestions?"

<u>Me</u> – "Umm . . . red jack on the black queen."

I feel a sudden urge to walk around with a sign saying, "Take the Bomb outta Bombay." And I will. Just as soon as this column finishes printing out.

Might as well play a little Solitaire 'til it does.

The Evening News

Unpublished

Good evening and welcome to Channel 963 News at 5, 6 and several other numbers. Jean is off tonight. We're not in sweeps, so John's in the Bahamas. Toni got lost coming back from our Salisbury newsroom and Frank is, shall we say, cosmetically challenged. I'm Lance Dentil. Here's tonight's Really Huge Story:

Channel 963 has learned that the Hornets are possibly moving to Terre Haute. In this exclusive interview with Abe and Francine Skilpepper of Weddington, Channel 963's Ermo Feldspar brings us up to date...

Um... we apologize for the technical difficulties. What Ermo reported was, the Skilpepper's, while visiting Abe's grandniece, allegedly saw George Shinn unloading crates of leftover #2 Larry Johnson jerseys from a teal colored Econoline van. Hornet officials could not be reached for comment, but several members of City Council vowed to get to the bottom of the report and get tougher in the negotiations for the new uptown arena. Channel 963 has also learned that Hornet's co-owner Ray Wooldridge has, in the past, allegedly ordered CD's from Columbia House Record Club, also based in Terre Haute. We'll continue to watch this story carefully.

Turning to the financial world, in tonight's "It's Just Small Change After All" segment, Money Reporter Gail Sales brings us the lowdown on the latest possible bank merger. Gail...

We... seem to be having some problems with our satellite truck. Gail would have reported that Charlotte-based First Union is allegedly getting ready to merge with Deutches Bank. Sources close to the bank have confirmed that bank president Ken Thompson was allegedly seen leaving the Little Professor Book Store with a complete version of the Berlitz "Two Weeks to Better German" tape course. The same sources have also divulged that Ed Crutchfield was allegedly observed dining at the Rheinland Haus, Heineken was allegedly served exclusively at the First Union awards dinner two week ago and many of the bank's tellers allegedly frequent nightclubs wearing lederhosen. Bank officials have not returned our phone calls, but several key members of the City Council used their cell phones to tell us they'll do everything in their power to get tough and line up another airline to open direct flights to Dusseldorf.

Turning to uptown construction, George Knute files this report on LCOR's plans for the old convention cent... ah, never mind. His equipment probably isn't working either and I can't stand the way he yells and flails his hands around. George did, however, uncover that LCOR would allegedly like the city to throw them a big party and pay to have festive ribbons tied on all the construction cranes. The one member of City Council we spoke to, who was not bending over backwards at the time, stated, "When we get tough, we get tough. We threatened to have a vote on character and look what happened to Slobodan Milosevic. Coincidence? I think not."

Coming up later on Channel 963 News, Biff Tucker on sports and his exclusive report on the Yankees allegedly moving to South End. 963 meteorologist Suzy Hale tells us about the real chance for a White Christmas, Easter and Fourth of July. And Andy Andrews is here with his hard hitting investigative report, "Rottweillers: Chihuahua Genetics Experiments Gone Bad." Stay with us.

Let's Make A Deal

Originally published April 16, 1999
© Charlotte Business Journal. All rights reserved.
Reprinted by permission

"Well, Mr. Smith, I'm sure you're going to enjoy your new car."

"Me, too."

"Yes, the Testosterone LXO Turbo Supremo is one of the hottest sport utility vehicles we sell here at Murple Motors and you got a great deal."

"Uh-huh."

"So, if you'll just sign these 240 documents, I'll hand you the keys and you can hit the road. They're standard purchase forms."

"Sure. And if you'll just sign this document, I'll sign your documents."

"What's this?"

"It's a standard advertising form."

"Advertising form? I don't understand..."

"Well, your detailing crew is, at this very moment, washing my T-LXO-TS SUV, filling the two forty-gallon gas tanks, tightening the hubcaps, buffing the Honey-Mustard Sparkle paint job to a patent leather luster..."

"Yes, of course..."

"...and putting the Murple Motors faux-chrome nameplate on the trunk lid."

"Yes. And...?"

"That's what this form is. It allows me to charge you for advertising on my car."

"Advertising?"

"That's what it's usually called when someone puts the name of a product or service in front of the public."

"We at Murple Motors know all about advertising, Mr. Smith. We have full page color ads in the paper every weekend. We run hundreds of radio commercials, louder and sillier than anyone else's. Why, we even put Mr. Murple in a nurse's costume, along with his pet Chihuahua in our TV spots. We know advertising.

"Yes and you also put your Murple Motors logo on my trunk. You've got a Murple Motors license plate frame on the back and a cardboard Murple Motors sign with a picture of the Chihuahua on the front, not to mention the complimentary Murple Motors key chain, visor sleeves, fuzzy dice, spare tire cover and the Murple Motors mud flaps."

"And what, pray, would a Testosterone LXO Turbo Supremo SUV be without mud flaps?"

"A shell of its former self, I'm sure. But do they have to have Murple on 'em?"

"Murple Motors has been a part of this town for 75 years, Mr. Smith. You should be honored to have the Murple name festooned on your bumper."

"Oh, I am, I am. But I'd be just as proud to have Apwanger Autos' aerial wind sock waving from the T-LXO-TS SUV I could buy from them."

"Apwanger agreed to this... this... advertising thing?"

"Yup."

"Alright. How much will it cost me?"

"Well, I figure ad panels on a city bus will run you about $2,000 a month and you get twenty buses. This is only one car, so that's about $100 a month."

"Too much. I can't afford it."

"Let's work with me here. I know you want to sell me that car."

"Yeah, yeah..."

"OK, so a Testosterone LXO is about the third the size of a bus, so divide $100 by three... that's $33.33. I'll eat the extra penny."

"Gosh, thanks."

"$33.33 per month for twelve months on a four year loan comes to..."

"One thousand five hundred ninety-nine dollars and eighty-four cents."

"Very good!"

"You want a check or to take it off the top?"

"Oh, let's just take it off the top."

"I'll sign this on two conditions."

"Name them."

"First, nobody and I mean *nobody* learns about this agreement."

"I can live with that."

"And secondly... do you think you could find out where Apwanger Autos got those aerial windsocks?"

"And if they have one that looks like a Chihuahua?"

"Bingo."

CEO Compensation Taxes My Math Skills

Originally published June 16, 2000
© Charlotte Business Journal. All rights reserved.
Reprinted with permission

I am not a mathematician. Oh, I can add a row of figures without too much smoke pouring from my ears. But as far as higher cipherin' goes, I was one of those kids who, when asked about the ratio of Sally's apples to Bobby's oranges would come up with an answer in kumquats, leaving my teachers shaking their heads, contemplating a more rewarding career in animal husbandry.

It's doubly disappointing for my dad who is an accountant and revels in neatly ordered columns of figures; a man to whom a balanced ledger holds a seamless beauty that rivals Chihuly glass and an argument won with the IRS is comparable to a first round KO of Mike Tyson. The fact that he sired a son who finds reconciling the checkbook something akin to a root canal and whose "5"'s look like "2"'s experiencing a bad flashback to some 1960's pharmaceutical encounter hasn't deterred him from his profession or made him love me any less. He still does my taxes.

So why venture into the realm of number crunching for this month's opus? A search for perspective.

CEO compensation is a hot topic right now. So hot that business publications have lists regarding what the Big Dawgs make. The most comprehensive listing I've found is in Business Week. To save you the time and probable boredom of doing this yourself, I've distilled a little breakdown:

First, for reference, the annual combined salaries for the U.S. Congress – based on an average of $137,000 per Senator and Representative – is $73,295,000. Compare that to the total annual pay (including long term compensation) for the top earner in the corporate ranks, Charles Wang, CEO of Computer Associates, Intl. – $655,424,000.

Allow me to crunch for ya. Mr. Wang's bottom line is about nine times that of the entire United States Congress. If Chuck were to get a weekly pay stub, he'd haul home $12,604,000.69 before taxes and FICA. To be fair, Mr. Wang doesn't get the highest base pay – only $4.6 million. Jack Welch of GE gets the blue ribbon with $13.3 million.

If you add up the annual comp for the Top 20 CEO's it comes to over $2.25 *billion*. If these gentlemen would allow us to shake the loose change out of their pockets and donate a mere 3.25 percent of their yearly haul, they could cover the Congressional paycheck and have more than $200,000 left over, enough to pay the President, if not his lawyers. And that's just for the Top 20 of the 361 CEO's listed. The average is about $3 million per Chief. That's another $1 billion, give or take a few drachmas. Granted, most of this wealth is on paper, but I doubt Charles Wang, Jack Welch or Michael Eisner would get turned down for a home equity loan.

What's the point of this? Is this a rallying cry for workers to rise up and smite the evil robber-barons.com? Is it a veiled hope that Charlie Wang has a secret, burning desire to build an uptown arena somewhere in the South (nudge, wink)? Nope. Just wanted to let Dad know I figured out most of the buttons on the calculator.

Charlotte Traffic? Try Chicago

Originally published May 28, 1999
© Charlotte Business Journal. All rights reserved.
Reprinted with permission

I just flew in from Chicago and – all together now – boy, are my arms tired. I made a day trip to the Windy City and fell in love. It's not the hometown, do-or-die, native "One Inch Thick Tar On Mah Heels" love I have for the Queen City. Perhaps it's more like respect; the respect and admiration you give an elderly uncle who is creased with the wisdom of age, yet still cool enough to have a tattoo, ride a Harley, sing opera and still have all his own teeth.

There are quite a few areas in which Charlotte and Chicago are similar. For instance, they both start with "Ch". And it gets better. Both cities are near a lake. Both cities' pro basketball teams want to be liked by Mike.

Charlotte wins the Tree competition. Chicago has the edge in old buildings. Our City Council (motto: We never met a developer we didn't like!) and the County Commission (motto: Ditto!) have seen to it we'll never have to bother with something musty like history or heritage in *our* downtown.

And although Charlotte's citizenry doesn't quite reach the tally of Chi-town's 3 million, the people there (and here) are, for the most part, extremely nice and the ratio of nice people to people who are jerks is about the same. Most sociologists will tell you that there is a slight downward, Charlotte-favoring skew in the all important Jerk Demographic, but that's mainly because of population curves.

But one area in which Chicago far outshines Charlotte is traffic. Listening to people here talk about driving, you'd think that every other city in America was Vehicular Nirvana, where speed limits are observed, traffic lights heeded and gentlemen drivers tip their hats to lady motorists and small children. But not here. In Charlotte, so goes conventional wisdom, our road rage makes center ring at the WWF look like a tea party. Cars are stacked up on I-77 and Independence like grocery carts in front of a Harris Teeter. *Why, it takes forty minutes just to drive across town*!

Try an hour and a half to get to the airport ten miles away. According to my driver, there *is* a lull in Chicago traffic from 11:30 A.M. 'til 1:15 P.M. when you can make it to O'Hare in about 70 minutes. And if it's raining? "All bets are off."

Believe me, you need a driver if you're from out of town. If you're not a native, tackling Chicago traffic without one is as dangerous as scaling Everest without a Sherpa. Heck, Chicago has bicycle delivery guys that could take on a tag team of our rudest redneck in his patchwork pick-up and an inconsiderate MBA in her cell phone- equipped Lexus and twist them into a Wrigley Field pretzel. But it wouldn't be malicious. That's just the way it is.

The moral to the story: as cities grow, so does the traffic. Get used to it. And if you want to complain to me about traffic in my beloved home town, first, go drive for an hour in Chicago. Then we'll talk.

After I landed, I hit the Billy Graham Parkway at 6:00 in the evening. After negotiating in and out of the Loop for a day, it was like a leisurely stroll around Freedom Park.

Defending My Right Not to Bare Chins

Originally published May 19, 2000
© Charlotte Business Journal. All rights reserved.
Reprinted with permission

I'm very fond of my beard.

I've had it, off and on (more on than off) since the heady days of my freshman collegiate year. I've bared my many-layered chin on few occasions, only for artistic expression (a dramatic presentation requiring a stubble-less face) or for capitalistic expression (a dramatic presentation that paid actual money). Which brings us to the National Rifle Association and Charleton Heston.

As you may have heard, Chuck and Crew will be in town for the NRA's national convention. So will numerous organizations that espouse varying levels of gun control. And the third interested party – the media – will be on the sidelines watching both like rabid meteorologists monitoring the confluence of two opposing air masses hoping for a storm of sound bites for their 6 PM packets.

Far be it from me to tread into the minefield of gun laws – at least in this journalistic incarnation – but I have a special place in my heart for Mr. Heston. He tried to save my beard.

Charlie's graced the Carolinas before. Years ago, he and his wife had a radio show in Hendersonville. And back in 1983, he and a cast of luminaries invaded Chester, South Carolina to make the TV movie "Chiefs". That is where the Fates brought the man who was Moses, Ben-Hur and the leather loincloth guy from Planet of the Apes – and my beard – together.

I was cast as a Klansman. Even had a line to say. Since it was the cross burning scene we waited until midnight to start shooting, the slow-waning summer light and a persnickety camera platform delaying things. After getting my hood from Wardrobe I was hustled to make-up by a young and energetic Assistant Director. (Understand, please, that on movie sets AD's are like ensigns on Star Trek. There's dozens of them and they're all expendable.) Wriggling past some towel draped person taking a nap in one of the makeup chairs, I submitted to a mussing of the hair and some Vaseline on my face. The AD reappeared, took one look at me and said, "Shave him."

A heated argument ensued, halted by a voice rumbling from beneath the towel – Charlton's. He gently asked the AD to go ask the director if it was absolutely necessary for me to shave. She was gone faster than a bullet from an NRA-sanctioned blunderbuss, only to come back and humbly inform Mr. Heston that, yes, the director deemed it mandatory. Chuck studied my face for a moment and said, "Tell you what. Why not just clip it down to stubble? You'll look more rustic and it won't take as long to grow back. Is that all right?"

I'm going to argue with Moses?

Thus de-bearded, I dove into my role. The shoot went on into the wee hours, a 45-second scene taking four hours to accomplish, fairly normal by Hollywood standards. My line ended up like my beard – on the cutting room floor. I never ran into Mr. Heston again. Perhaps I'll saunter down to the Convention Center and see if I can sneak in and corner him next to the shrimp boat at the buffet. Not to discuss politics or pistols.

Just to show him it did grow back.

Even a Lawsuit Tastes Better When It Sits on a Ritz

Originally published January 29, 1999
© Charlotte Business Journal. All rights reserved.
Reprinted with permission

The legal battle of the century is underway.

The impeachment trial in the Senate? Not hardly. The Government v. Gates? Hah! A John Grisham reject in comparison. Even the clash between America On Line and anybody who can form simple sentences over the ownership of "You've got mail" pales in contrast. No, nothing less important hangs in the balance of the judicial probity of our federal courts than the fate of . . .

Fish crackers.

That's crackers shaped like fish, not New and Improved Salted Tuna Treats.

In this corner, wearing the white and gold trunks with the fancy script writing on the waistband, the champion Fish Cracker company, maker of the genuine world-famous Goldfish ® crackers . . . Pepperidge Farm! (Please pronounce that, "Pep-ridge Fahm, a-yuh.")

In the other corner, fighting in the conglomerate division, wearing the red trunks covered in those funny little ovals with the TV antennas on 'em, maker of more snacks than you can shake a pretzel stick at . . . Nabisco!

Touch oven mitts and come out slugging.

It seems Nabisco has gotten in the promotional bed with a new kids' cartoon show in which the main character is half-cat and half-dog and is redesigning its Cheez Nips product to tie in with the program. In an amazing logical leap, Nabisco feels that part of the cracker combination should represent the favorite snack of the cat-half cracker, hence the fish cracker. (The immediate question to be raised is whether or not they'll include a mailman-shaped cracker for the canine half.)

Pepperidge Farm howled like a harpooned humpback and threatened to sue, saying it has a trademark on the "Goldfish configuration" and that Nabisco was trying to muddy the snack food waters, confusing the poor guppy-gullible public with a false fish promise they'd swallow hook, line and . . . never mind.

Nabisco's restraint lasted about as long as a bag of Oreos at a Grateful Dead concert. In a preemptive strike, they did file suit, asking the court to pooh-pooh Pepperidge Farm's trademark claims and say that the fish shape is "generic" and anybody with some flour, water and some No. 3 Red Dye should be able to whip out a batch of crunchy cod-like crackers.

This is important stuff, folks. What if just any cracker mogul decided to leap on the marine munchie band-wagon? Upstart, upscale stone-ground designer crackers would appear in the shape of tiny mahi-mahi. Frito-Lay might start selling a spicy salsa-flavored crackers in the form of piranha: the cracker that bites back. Imagine the marketplace pandemonium if Keebler should loose its elfin magic and come out with Salmon Snaks with Li'l Pointy Ears. It'd make the Crash of '29 look like a tailgate party.

According to facts found on their respective web sites, the cracker market coveted by both companies is more than just a quiet place to park your Brie. Nabisco, with over two hundred brands under its umbrella – including crackers, cereals and Milk Bone dog biscuits (now, why not put those in with Cat/Dog?) – produces a billion and a half pounds of cookies and crackers a year. That's a lotta Lorna Doones, kids. And Pepperidge Farm, a division of Campbell Soup Co. pops out over one million Goldfish an hour, supplying one out of three American households with the lucrative demographic of children ages 2 to 12 with mega-bags of the tasty Osteichthyes. This is not a silly tiff over a few crumbs.

But in this case, as in most where corporate giants have a go at each other, it's the consumer that ends up paying the legal fees. That's why your next box of Shredded Wheat might cost $24. Unless, of course, the firms representing Nabisco and Pepperidge Farm would consider taking their pay in Snak-Wells and seasoned stuffing mix. Watch this paper, Court TV and perhaps the next episode of "Fishing with Orlando" for updates.

Dear Santa@ northpole.com

Originally published December 28, 1998
© Charlotte Business Journal. All rights reserved.
Reprinted with permission

Dear Santa,

This is the first time I've written to you since I was in the third grade. I feel it is necessary. The gifts you selected for me last year weren't quite what I had in mind. Nothing personal, but the floating, beeping golf balls and the $10 Rogaine certificate seemed a bit sarcastic from a jolly old elf like yourself. And I don't really care how good a deal you got on those Kerry Collins Panther jerseys. I've been a good boy, so here are few suggestions.

I'd like more work. This year has been good, but I could always be busier. I'm really glad I'm self-employed since lately corporations have handed out more pink slips than Victoria's Secret. I've got some spare time on my hands because of the NBA lockout. No announcing for the pros, but I am doing a high school tournament at the end of the month. Yes, there are high school basketball players who weren't drafted last year. Imagine, Santa. The buses those kids arrive in cost as much as Patrick Ewing makes in one game. Heck, maybe the first half. And I think the owners deserve a big lump of coal in their stockings, too... oops. I forgot. Marv Albert is already broadcasting again.

I'd really like some new toys. You know the kind of stuff I like, but there are a few I'd like you to avoid, if possible:

the House Judiciary Committee Board Game

the Jack Kervorkian autographed edition of "Operation™"

the Radical Evangelist Environmentalist Doll with the protest sign that says "Club Homos, Not Seals"

the "I-485 at 5:00 "Action Race Car Set

the "Coming Out" Barbie™ and Ken™ with the Designer Closet and Judge's Robe the Tickle Me Janet Reno

I know there's a back order for the Spookee™ Kenneth Starr Talking Special Prosecutor. I've heard it's just a question of which sentence they pick for its pull-string is scarier: "I'm here with a subpoena" or "I need more money for my investigation." And, yes, I'm a technology buff, but finding a Linda Tripp Answering Machine under the tree would be as much fun as a Furby with laryngitis.

A few gifts you might consider for other good boys and girls:

a Whistler Key chain for Eric Rudolph. Then the FBI could walk through the North Carolina mountains whistling Dixie and home right in on him. (If he's hiding down at the Citadel, they'll have to whistle something else.)

For Erskine Bowles, a box of Ric Flair for Governor campaign buttons. Hey, if it's good enough for Jessie Ventura...

If the kids at NASA have been good, let their Mars Climate Orbiter satellite find ice on the Red Planet. If they've been *real* good let 'em find a single malt scotch, too.

I just got a new computer, so no need to worry about that. If I have any technical questions I'll just get council member Tim Sellers to talk to God for me. I could use some ink cartridges for my printer. I've been doing quite a bit of writing lately and they last about as long as a new sitcom on the Fox Network. Speaking of writing, I was considering asking for one of those voice activated word processing programs. I saw one being demonstrated at one of the big media stores. But they left it on next to a TV that had a show with Fran Drescher talking and the application erased itself, kind of a digital hara-kiri. And if you could, have the folks at Disney look at my full-length animated movie script. It's about a real short pro basketball player who gets turned into an ant and saves the colony. I call it "A Bogues' Life".

Well, that's all I can think of for this year, Santa. I just want this to be a good old-fashioned, traditional Yuletide. If I come up with anything else, I'll e-mail you.

Merry Christmas!
James K.

Credit Where Credit is Due

Originally published August 6, 1999
© Charlotte Business Journal. All rights reserved.
Reprinted with permission

To paraphrase Andy Worhol, every fifteen minutes somebody gets a credit card application. It's probably more like every fifteen nano-seconds. There are urban legends, excuse me, *plastic* legends about people who have received credit cards for their dead relatives, live pets and certain house plants that they've named. (They are *select* house plants, though, plants that know the value of good credit and based on their excellent botanical credit rating, who knows? Maybe a well established philodendron does deserve $50,000 and a sheet of instant access checks.)

This is not to bemoan the random acquisition of billions of dollars by the general public (at prime plus 23%), but to salute the cagey marketers of those little specialty squares of promised monetary magic, the ones I like to call DP's. Demographic Plastics.

You know. You've gotten an application for one. "Dear Mr. Spwzchikoskowzc. The proud heritage of all the Spwzchikoskowzcs world wide can now open the door to your new BancPlas Spwzchikoskowzc Magnesium Card..."

"...and as one of the proud, select owners of a miniature whiskerless Tibetan puma, we're proud to offer you the new Plutonium Tibetan Puma Card..."

"...as an insatiable gardener, you can get up to 6 trillion dollars on your new Berkelium Aphid Card..."

Berkelium is an actual element. Makes you wonder what's going to happen to credit when they reach the end of the periodic chart. Probably move back into the gases. Great! You'll get a Helium card with balloon payments. Ba-da-bump.

I have received card offers from financial entities that pandered to my last name, my college, the fact that I own a dachshund and most recently because I'm a science fiction buff. This latest proposal grants me a choice of five, count 'em, five different full color facades guaranteed to get my little sci-fi heart a'pumpin'. One is fairly normal, a picture of a bright sun and a panoply of stars. Two feature glowing space ships on cards that must do everything except phone home. One spotlights Stonehenge (the new Druid Gold card? Don't leave the solstice without it.) And the last depicts a long fingered, shadowy figure which is either an alien or some guy from a collection agency going for your wallet.

The only one of these I was suckered . . . um, wisely invested in was one that offered me a chance to be on the first commercial flight into space if I got the card. I'll never use it to buy anything. (I learned my credit card lesson after college. Can you say, "righteous stereo system, dude"? Ten years later, it was paid off.) There's no annual fee on my Trip to Space DP. I'll hang on to it until I find out I'm not going into orbit, then cancel it. It's the same thing I do with all those "Try One Issue of Our Magazine" offers. I get the invoice, scrawl "cancel" on it and get two or three issues before their computer figures out I'm not going to pony up for a subscription.

Is this a great country or what?

In the meantime, keep an eye out for your Science Fiction credit card. Helpful hint: don't send in the application signed Scully Mulder. You'll be getting junk mail under that name until Y3K.

Alex Forever

Unpublished

The annals of marketing have produced more famous promises than a C-130 full of politicians. "Whiter whites!" "More taste!" "You'll love New Coke!" Now we can add to the list, "Immortality." (Notice the lack of an exclamation mark. This wise marketer doesn't stoop to hyperbole.)

Welcome to the world of Alex. I won't give his last name or tell you his web address. If you're that interested, you'll hunt him up yourself. I stumbled across Alex's ad in the back of Popular Science, snuggled amongst the ads for mind controllers, cybernetic ears and "Secret Forbidden Knowledge of Anti-Gravity". There are also half a dozen or so ads for cable box descramblers, but I won't get on my soapbox about those. Not now, at least.

No, let's focus on good ol' Alex, who has a gizmo... actually several gizmos (gizmies?) that will let you stick around to see if we survive Y3K. The Eternal Life Foot Braces and Finger Rings can be yours, friends, for the amazingly low price of $105 American. And that includes shipping. All major credit cards and COD's accepted. Such a deal!

The rings pictured in the ad could be recycled Mood Rings from the '70's. The Foot Braces look like something from the Torquemada Page on E-Bay. The idea is that the magnets in the rings and braces speed up your circulation, making your blood work better and thus nourish and youthen (is that a word?) your body. And bless his little pumped-up arteries, satisfaction is assured by Alex, although I wonder what this satisfaction could be. Your toes don't fall off? If you ever do kick the bucket your estate can sue Alex? Why not? I imagine he's using his own product and he'd still be around. I'd love to hear *that* closing argument. "And, members of the jury, even if my client had not been hit by that bus on his 178th birthday, would his Foot Braces have performed as well?"

While Alex does assure satisfaction, he does hedge his bet earlier in the ad by saying his invention "is believed" to stop the aging process.

Smart move, Alex.

Part of me says, let's not be too hasty. Heck, they laughed at Orville and Wilbur. Everybody's got a story about a relative that passed on silly start-up companies like International Business Machines and Microsoft. I could get some Life Braces, try 'em out and still be writing this when Halley's comet comes back. And I could write off the cost as research expense... nah.

Well, best of luck there, Big A. Your ad and your web site make you sound very sincere. Some people might want to live forever. I don't. And like George Carlin said, "You nail together two things that have never been nailed together before, some (one) will buy it from you." But if there are folks out there that are willing to part with a C-note to magnetize their tootsies, I can't think of anyone I'd rather get the money.

But, gosh. Right next to Alex's ad is... the Amazing Laser Window Listener for just $40 bucks more. Ooooh!

I'm a sucker for good marketing.

Business Humor

(This column was a pitch to the Business Editors of the Charlotte Observer in 2005. It never saw the light of day.)

So, this CFO walks into a bar with a pig under his arm. Somebody says, "Where'd you get that?" The pig says, "I got him as part of the merger package."

A humor column is not something you'd expect to see in the business section of the newspaper.

That was no lady. That was my joint filing partner.

Business and money are serious subjects, especially in this town. There are a bunch of tall buildings here, none of which are multi-story comedy clubs.

... but this one's eating my prospectus!

But considering the tenor of the business community for the last four years, it's hard to think of any other group that needs cheering up more than those that crunch numbers for a living. That's not to say that bankers, stock brokers, et al, can't be party animals. There are unsubstantiated and non-confirmable rumors that a recent board meeting of a prestigious financial institution turned into a pie fight worthy of Laurel and Hardy. (I'm not at liberty to say where it was, but if you see Ken Lewis, I'd steer clear of the words "lemon meringue".)

So, the Charlotte Observer editors, in their never ending quest to stay on the cutting edge of journalistic trends are going to let me take a whack at business humor. The approach isn't as outlandish as you may believe. Example: *Enron* and *Leno* have many of the same letters. Coincidence? I think not.

And I am perfectly suited for the task. I've won a North Carolina Press Association Award for humor columns. I was reasonably funny on a daily basis while in radio. And watching me balance my checkbook makes Robin Williams looks like Alan Greenspan.

Also, at the moment, there is a comedy vacuum in print journalism. Dave Barry is on an extended hiatus. While Dave didn't dwell specifically on business humor, he was at the top of his craft and his waggery made its way to all classes of the humor-depleted; kind of a trickle-down theory of humor.

"Jokel-down", if you will. Other wits, like the Observer's own Doug Robarchek, will be expected to take up the slack. To place all of this tremendous burden on poor Doug seems unfair, at least until the tests come back and they can up his "medication". The solution, then, is to specialize humor. There could be a satirist for all sections of the paper. Why, the sports section alone begs for a DH (Designated Humorist.)

You may still be asking, though, why business humor? How can it benefit the public? And how can it benefit the economics of a newspaper? The answer to the first question is rudimentary. Laughter heals. It knows no ethnic or age boundaries. *Funny* crosses all language barriers. A good joke is the print equivalent of the Euro. (See? Another business reference. It's a natural!)

The second question is just as easy to answer. Newspapers are always looking for new and exciting ways to increase readership. And a business humor column will draw readers to the business section that normally wouldn't be caught dead here; i.e. – young people. It won't be long before the standard greeting between CEOs will be "Yo, dawg." A zippy little sobriquet for this column like "BizHum" will have Gen X through Z scanning the Amex and NASDAQ like they were scrolling through their Ipods looking for Nellie. It beats the alternative. I shouldn't tell you this, but before I approached the editors, they were flirting with trying to reach the all important 18-25 demographic with a column called "Pimp My Portfolio". It wasn't pretty.

So, we're off. I'll do my best to keep you abreast of the business world in a way that is just a teensy bit tangential. We'll tie together government, science, education and the arts with a big ol' business bow. Put some fun back in your funds.

And if I can, just once on an early Monday morning, make some drowsy, young executive sitting in Starbucks do a spit-take with his double latte, I'll consider my job well done.

Science Quiz 2000

Originally published July 21, 2000
© Charlotte Business Journal. All rights reserved.
Reprinted with permission

Time for our semi-regular science quiz. Put your books under your desk, your laptops off your laps and make sure all your palm pilots are cleared for landing. As usual it's true/false. There's no time limit but remember . . . no wagering. Here we go.

1. Scientists can grow mouse teeth.

True. And it's not being underwritten by Michael Eisner. Researchers at the Texas Health Science Center in San Antonio have isolated certain mouse cells, including dentin and enamel, that when mixed with the right chemicals grow mouse teeth. The process can hopefully be used on humans . . . to grow human teeth, not mousey ones. Imagine trying to chow down on a t-bone at Mortons with chompers the size of thumb tacks. That's exciting news for the estimated 113 million U.S. citizens who are missing at least one tooth. It's twice as exciting for all those mice who shell out monthly for Efferdent. In related news, the Tooth Fairy was seen picketing the Texas Health Science Center.

2. Bio-magnetic shoes can improve circulation.

Sorry. Trick question. I don't know if it's true or false. There are thousands, though, who swear that magnets do everything from get your blood moving to relieve arthritis. That's what Florsheim Shoes is betting on. It's paying off. Last year Florsheim sold 70,000 pairs of MagneForce golf shoes at $120 a pop and they expect to double that this year. There's no scientific proof that magnets help any ailment, but science also said bumblebees can't fly. And even if magnetic golf shoes don't make your feet feel better or improve your game, it makes it a darn sight easier to pick up your putter.

3. Grocery carts are alive and attack car fenders for food.

False. But science has come up with a way to keep carts from ending up as someone's home garden wagon. Gatekeeper Systems has a wheel device that locks when it passes over a wire buried in the parking lot, kind of like the collar that keeps Rover in your yard. An electronic key unlocks the wheels so they can be pushed back where they belong: blocking the parking space closest to the door.

4. Babies can learn a foreign language at 10 months.

True. At least that's when they start tuning into whatever language they're around the most. Hence *The Babbler* from Neurosmith. This plush, smiley crescent moon toy with star push buttons lets your budding linguist hear sounds in Spanish, French and Japanese. The company contends it'll make it easier for Baby to learn the languages. I hope the video camera is rolling when, instead of "Mama, Dada" Junior's first words are "Domo arigato, mademoiselle."

5. You could be wrapping your next present with gecko feet.

True. Granted, it would put an interesting wrinkle in gifts under the Christmas tree this year, but since geckos can climb anything and anywhere, biologists and engineers at U-Cal at Berkeley have been studying the feet of Tokay geckos. And they discovered . . . fly swatters. Or submicroscopic hairs shaped like fly swatters – billions of 'em – that allow the gecko's toes to bond with surfaces without excreting any sticky stuff. The application? Tape that could seal under water and in the vacuum of space. Watch for Scotch Magic Transparent Gecko Feet® at an Office Max near you.

All right. Pencils down. Leave an apple for the teacher . . . just as long as it isn't genetically altered.

Did You File Your Form 10-Pharaoh?

Unpublished

From the Associated Press: Clay tablets discovered in southern Egypt – dating back 5,300 years – are thought to be ancient Egyptian tax records. They record linen and oil deliveries made as a tithe to King Scorpion I.

"Have a seat, please. Mr. Ahmed."
"Thank you."
"Is this your first visit to our nation's capital?"
"No, but it's my first visit to the IRS."
"There's no need to be nervous, Mr. Ahmed."
"Sorry, but this is also my first audit."
"Please. We here at the Isis Revenue Service have been commanded by King Scorpion to be more friendly and sympathetic."
"Tell that to my brother-in-law, Qizmet. You guys attached his camels."
"Not every case is the same, sir."
"It's scary enough paying taxes to a king named Scorpion."
"I understand. We do appreciate you coming all the way to Cairo from your home in Luxor."
"And I thought I'd paid my luxor-y tax. HAHAHAHaha ha . . . heh . . . ahem . . . just a little tax joke."
"Yes. Now, let's look at your return."
"It's in that wheelbarrow over there."
"Wheelbarrow?"
"Hey, clay tablets are heavy. I didn't know if 1099 was the form number or the weight."
"Well, sir, if you filed the short form and didn't itemized . . . "

"I'd owe you twice as much. I can't afford it. Do you know what my barge rates were for shipping just Schedule C this far north?"

"You could take advantage of new technology."

"That's what my former accountant says. Notice I said 'former'. He's all hot about this gizmo called an abacus. Ha! Counting beads on a rack. Next thing you know, he'll be using this new papyrus stuff instead of clay."

"You could use our new on-line filing system."

"On-line? How does that work?"

"We run a line of slaves to your house and they pass your tablets down the line to the collection center."

"Nah. I'm afraid I lose something in the transmission. What if they drop a tablet?"

"True, there are still a few bugs in the system."

"Bugs?"

"Locusts, in particular."

"Oh."

"Not to worry. Most of your return is in fine shape. There's only a few flagged items I'd like to ask you about. Let's see . . . hmmm. You've got a pretty hefty deduction for chariot expenses. Is your chariot strictly for business use?"

"Oh, yeah. I'm a traveling linen and oil salesman. I put quite a few miles on the ol' buggy for business. It's all in the expense log."

"In the wheelbarrow?"

"Yup."

"This client listed in Memphis . . . um, I'm sorry. I can't read your hieroglyphics. "

"Ah . . . yeah. That would be 'Qizmet'."

"Your brother-in-law?"

"Yes. Is there a problem?"

"I thought you said he was in camels."

"Yeah, he is. 'Memphis Qizmet, the Walking Egyptian's Friend.' So what?"

"I thought you were in linens and oils."

"Hey, can I help it if Qizmet wants the best dressed, slickest camels in Egypt?"

"I see. Moving on to the next flagged item. I'm afraid I'm going to have to disallow this dependent deduction for housing for your mother.

"No, no, no. Heh-heh, my rotten hand-glyphing again. That's a business deduction. For storage of my mummy. You know. At one of those self-storage pyramids? They've got those big signs out front with the funny hieroglyphs on 'em? 'Honk if you love King Scorpion'. 'It's Not Sweat, You're in De Nile'. 'We Store Everything Including the Kitchen Sphinx'. That sort of thing."

"Storage for your mummy."

"It's not really a family member. It's a demo mummy. The linen I sell is the finest mummification wrap in the Nile Delta. It's a business expense. I've got some swatches here . . . "

"That won't be necessary."

"I've got the receipts in the wheelbarrow."

"I'm sure you do. Perhaps we can let that one slide. Just one final question, Mr. Ahmed. I notice you have a write-off here for a fairly large purchase listed as office supplies.

"Oh, yeah. Office supplies."

"From the Osiris Home and Garden Center?"

"It's a legitimate business expense!"

"How so?"

"What, you think clay for all these tablets grows on trees? I'm a busy man. I can't run down to the river bank for some mud every time I need an invoice or the IRS needs a new form. I have to buy the ready-mix."

"Very well. But that's not the total bill. What's this other charge for?"

"Oh. That's for the wheelbarrow."

"I see."

Pixie Dust at the Bargaining Table

Originally published September 15, 2000
© Charlotte Business Journal. All rights reserved.
Reprinted with permission

The most recent acquisition target in this merger-manic economy is Keebler Foods, owned by Flowers Industries, Inc. The cookie and cracker maker is being examined by Kellogg's, Danone SA, Campbell Soup Co., Quaker Oats Co. and H.J. Heinz Co. The Business Journal has scored a reportorial coup by interviewing the president of the No. 2 snack company, Ernie Keebler. What follows is an excerpt:

BJ – What's the current mood at Keebler?

EK – Fairly upbeat, I must say. Of course a deal's a good way off, but in any takeover situation there are going to be some nervous moments. We've been assured there will be very few changes no matter who buys us.

BJ – Are you looking for anything in particular in a potential buyer?

EK – A strong bottom line, historical consistency, good P/E ratio and a fundamental understanding of magic.

BJ – Um . . . magic?

EK – Any product that is manufactured by elves in a magic oven takes a certain level of belief in the paranormal. That's not something that normally impacts negotiations in the run-of-the-mill acquisition. Any bumpkin corporation with a bunch of night-school MBA's at the helm can take us over, but one that understands the nuances linking marketing and magic . . . heck, the balance between inventory control and pixie dust alone boggles the mind. We aren't looking for some Tinkerbell-come-lately, you know.

BJ – We can imagine. Any attractive qualities in the five that are considering bidding?

EK – They all have their strong points. Kellogg has a great history. I'm not sure how the management structure would pan out. They're kind of heavy in their upper echelons.

BJ – So some top level managers would be let go?

EK – There'd be some weeding out. Not sure whether it'd be Snap, Crackle or Pop, but the severance stock offer would be substantial, whoever it was. And I'd stay on as COE.

BJ – You mean CEO.

EK – No, COE. Chief Operating Elf. (Laughs) Beside, I need the job. Just closed on a new hollow tree in Central Park West.

BJ – Uh-huh. What about the other companies?

EK – Quaker Oats is good. Strong sales. Trading price is up there. Gatorade is doing well for them. Campbell's already has Pepperidge Farm, so Soup Boy is a long shot. Not sure about Heinz. They've got that green ketchup thing going on. And who the heck knows what Danone SA markets?

BJ – Yogurt and Evian water.

EK – Hmm . . . elfin fudge-striped yogurt . . . Nah, can't see it.

BJ – Do you foresee any major changes after the sale?

EK – We'll do everything humanly possible to make sure the transition is a pleasant and fair one for all our employees.

BJ – "Humanly possible"? Mr. Keebler, you're an elf.

EK – So?

BJ – You don't think that could effect your company's value?

EK – Not in the long run. Two months ago there was a rumor going around that Alan Greenspan was a leprechaun. Caused a slight correction. No big deal.

BK – So you see any acquisition as . . . ?

EK – Uncommonly good. Want a box of Hi-Ho's?

BJ – Thank you, no.

SouthPark – TV or Not TV?

Originally published September 10, 1999
© Charlotte Business Journal. All rights reserved.
Reprinted with permission

South Park

A name that stirs fear in the hearts of parents. Foul-mouthed. Crude. Socially and politically incorrect. A magnet for pre- and post-pubescent youngsters looking to rebel against authority. But enough about the mall's Food Court on a Saturday night. Let's talk about the movie.

No, seriously. I love SouthPark. The mall, not the TV show or the movie. As one of the few remaining Charlotte natives, I grew up witnessing this grand mall and business micro-metropolis rise almost phoenix-like from the once bucolic cow pastures of southeast Charlotte. I have shopped its cruciform corridors. I have done radio broadcasts from beside its sparkling fountain with its penny-spangled depths. And yes, I have circled for hours in my car at Christmas trying to time it juust right and get a parking space underneath near the escalators. I have lived SouthPark, the mall.

I haven't seen the movie. It quietly left the theaters before I was asked to write this piece and for some strange reason hasn't made it to the $1.50 screens. (Can you say, "there's more money in video rentals?") But South Park (the show, not the mall) is a cultural phenomenon. Hey, it's been on the cover of "People". Its popularity then begs the question, has there been any backlash from this ribald bit of Americana that has hurt the image of Charlotte's first mega-mall? The Business Journal wanted to know. So, if the "movin' pitcher" is out of the equation and information isn't forthcoming from watching Comedy Central, where can a serious journalist like me go for the real story?

The Internet. And my 17 year old son's friends.

South Park (the TV show, not the mall) for those of you who may be blissfully unaware, is the brainchild of Coloradans Matt Stone and Trey Parker. The animated paper cutout show debuted on Comedy Central in 1997 after what their bios call "a good old fashioned Hollywood bidding war." Its popularity expanded following a few raves from film festivals and a vast underground – i.e., Internet – distribution of a short film (originally produced as a video yuletide greeting for one of the Fox moguls) called "Spirit of Christmas" featuring the SP regulars: ring leader Kyle, the fat, foul-mouthed Cartman, the ever-doomed Kenny (he gets killed in every episode), et al. They witness a battle between Santa Claus and Jesus. It's filthy, sacrilegious to a fair-the-well and... funny. Yeah, I laughed at it. So sue me. The amazing thing is that Stone and Parker have managed to clean up the original idea enough even for the relaxed rules of cable.

The Internet search furnished me with hundreds of pages all dedicated to South Park – the TV show, not the mall. There was only one hit that came close to being mall-oriented and that was for SouthPark Toastmasters, whose members, if they were to speak like Cartman, would be cease being Toastmasters and simply become toast. There were only a couple of "official" sites offered by the movie company and Comedy Central. The other gazillion URLs were personal sites set up by people who desperately need to seek a life or competent medical attention. Still, the so-called Information Highway yielded no data on what, if any, effect the show has had on the mall. Where to turn?

Teenagers.

Teenagers, rebellious media and malls go together like peanut butter, jelly and Quick Fried Cheetos. My son and his friends are good kids, but when we budding Bernsteins are in pursuit of a story, we can't let blood ties or good neighborliness stand in the way of the truth. After softening them up with a few easy questions like, "Have you seen the show?" and "Have you ever been to the mall?" I hit 'em with the hard question like a blackjack against their noggins on a dark and stormy night. "Um, you guys think there's any negative correlation between the mall and the show?"

"No."

Too late. They're wise to me.

Punks.

So, as a last resort, I turn to the one person who can give me a definitive answer: the director of SouthPark Mall.

Diane Ballard is the Mall Director for Faison-owned SouthPark and a very enjoyable person to talk to. She knows her mall; the history, the customers, the merchants. After some disarming banter about SouthPark's past and future, I hurled the main question at her like a Greg Maddux fastball.

Her response? "Oh. Well, when it first came on a couple of people called to ask how we could sponsor a show like that. But there hasn't been much more since." Her candor and cordial manner made me ditch my other two questions about the possibility of a South Park SouthPark store, perhaps next to the Disney or Warner Bros. stores and the rather obvious question as to whether anyone with Faison looks like Cartman.

We professional journalists know where to draw the line.

A Dollar By Any Other Name

Unpublished

"The continent is just abuzz with this new currency, Daphne. I tell you, designer money is going to be the next hot statement. Simply everybody is going to have their own legal tender. Pardon, Stephanie? Oh . . . three hearts. Forgive me.

"No, Buxton came home from the brokerage one night last week, poor dear, barely had the strength to ask the au pair to send kisses up to Buxy, Jr. what with all this up and down so close to 11,000 and trading in his T-bills for amazon.com shares and . . . oh, um . . . four clubs . . . where was I? Oh, yes and he said, 'Mavica, this euro is getting ready to take off'. Those were his very words, Marcia – 'take off' – and it started me into thinking: if those silly little European countries can have their own money, why can't we?

"Oh, I know we have our own for the United States, silly, but why can't we have our own personal money. I mean, the dollar is nice and all, but the name just plods, simply plods off the tongue. Not like 'euro'. Isn't it sweet? Sounds like one of those little sports cars, like the one Hughbly Comstack bought for that trophy wife of his. What, dear? Oh, no, no, No! . I think our money is just fine, but if we don't act soon all the good names are going to be taken.

"Buxton thinks I'm being just mega-silly, but I'll bet, right now, that silly little country that has that darling little man with the donkey delivering the coffee beans is trying to trademark 'burro'. I can just imagine doctors getting together and demanding they be paid in 'cure-os'. Buxton said network news shows might ask advertisers to spend 'murrows'... whatever that means. And those silly farmers would probably want to trademark 'furros' for their money. Furros. You know, 'furrows'? Farmers? Didn't your hubby attend State? It is an agricultural school, isn't it? Never mind, Daphne, dear, that's your trick . . .

"What, dear? No, Stephanie, I think lawsuits settled for jur-o's is taking it a step too far. But sadly, that won't stop some people from over-reaching. Gardeners working for barrows, fencing club members paying dues in zorros, surrealist artists asking outrageous prices for their canvases in miros. Why, it would only be a matter of time before we'd go to our favorite Greek restaurant and pay for our souvlaki in gyros, for pity's sake.

"No, Marcia, I don't think it will stop there. Ask for a loan at the bank and get 'borrows'. Purchasing Agatha Christie mysteries with 'poirots'. Buxton mentioned something about buying a pair of those ghastly overalls using 'jethros' . . . Sometimes I have no idea what he's talking about.

"In fact, he doesn't take me seriously at all. He teased me mercilessly yesterday morning after I explained this to him. He laughed all the way through his breakfast latte, spraying bran muffin crumbs everywhere. 'We could get our Valentine's cards with arrows!' he scoffed. "Hire a lawyer with darrows!' and then mentioned something about tickets for some silly Sixties folk group music concert bought with yarrows. And he calls himself a financial advisor!

"I'm sorry, dears. Thank you. It's silly to get so upset. Let's just play. I won't even think of Buxton, I just won't.

"My bid?"

"Clubs."

TV Sweeps Appeal to Greed

Originally published November 19, 1999
© Charlotte Business Journal. All rights reserved.
Reprinted with permission

Here's two words that should strike fear in the hearts of all Americans: Regis Philbin.

Game shows are back and bigger than ever. And I'm not referring to perennials like Jeopardy and Wheel of Fortune. These new shows don't let contestants scan Vanna for a "Q" while half-heartedly chanting "big money, big money" or kindly ask Alex, "Zygotes for $200, please". Nah, these programs make Gordon Gecko look like St. Francis. "Who Wants To Be A Millionaire" and "Greed" are the shows the networks hope will be the ratings' floggers during November sweeps. The payoff for participants? Money. Lots of money. And maybe the home version of *Greed* and a couple of boxes of Rice-a-Roni.

To win, competitors have to answer questions. The first round questions – for paltry sums – are easy. "For $5, Phil, what is your favorite color?" They get tougher as the pot grows. "For $10, Phil, what is the name of the pet cockatiel that belongs to the tribesman who lives at the headwater of the Zambalaqwesi River?" (It's a trick question. The answer, of course, is it's not a cockatiel, but a macaw called Elmer.) But considering the amount of cash on the line, asking questions is all these shows demand of their participants. "Only" you may ask? What else could be the focus of a game show?

Let's go to France and tune in "Fort Boyard". Contestants are transported to an old French island fort somewhere in the Atlantic and have to battle "semi-supernatural" figures clad in latex. The bad news is the in-flight film is Papillon.

Tonight on the Bangkok Channel, it's "Lachapor Khun Ru Chai", where a celebrity guest is confronted with three embarrassing details from his or her life. Their friends (at least *before* the show they're friends) have to guess which one the celebrity regrets the most.

Let's aim the satellite dish at Spain and pick an episode of "Grand Prix" and watch two village teams, with their mayors as captains, compete for prizes. The clip I saw had the mayor dressed up as a large, fuzzy egg dodging a young bull. I don't care how many votes he got, let's see Pat McCrory try *that* one.

And finally, a twist of the dial brings us to Germany and "Strip". No, it's not a quiz show on comics. Competing co-ed teams answer questions about sex while lithe disco dancers disrobe. The producers, bless their hearts, offer picture clues for the more difficult questions. The losing team strips. And gets a few boxes of Rice-a-Roni. "Strip" would be a revenue winner in the States. Imagine all the potential sponsorships from plastic surgery clinics.

Keep these shows in mind. After all, "Who Wants To Be A Millionaire" was an import from jolly old England. The next time your index finger gets a cramp from punching the channel button on the remote don't gripe. Settle for "The Crocodile Hunter Meets the Rugrats". If you wish for something new to watch . . . you may get it.

Hornets Insider? Not Exactly

Originally published March 24, 2000
© Charlotte Business Journal. All rights reserved.
Reprinted with permission

Down at the end of this column is a short biographical statement that tells you a little bit about me. I'll wait a second while you read it. Hmmm . . . hmmm . . . hm, hm, hm . . . there. Nice to have forty-five years of your life summed up in twelve words (eleven if you count "Charlotte-based" as one 'cause it's hyphenated, but why split grammatical hairs.)

I'd like to update this mini-resume. Please add, in your choice of writing utensil, assistant Cub Scout Den Leader and public address announcer for the Hornets.

Yep, I'm the guy that yells, "Heeeeere come your Hornets!" and "Heeere come your HoneyBees!" and "Heere comes some t-shirts!" and "here comes the pudgy guy to do a back flip," although we haven't seen Flipper (his nom de flip) this season. And they wonder why attendance is down. But I digress . . .

I bring this up for three reasons. A) It's fun and I enjoy it. B) I like people to know I *actually get paid real money* for *watching* a basketball game and C) because of the pending presentation to Queen City leaders on building a new arena uptown. Time for a Business Journal Scoop and publically spill the nachos on everything I know about the proposed plan. Here it is in a nutshell:

Nothing.

I don't know anything. I haven't seen any plans. I haven't been asked to any budget meetings. I've met Ray Wooldridge a total of four times and while he's a pleasant fellow he has yet to pull me aside to ask me how I think Lynn Wheeler is going to vote.

Likewise, Paul Silas has yet to ask me whether he should call a high pick-and-roll or throw it into the low post. The last suggestion I made even resembling that was "a high Pic-n-Pay" and you see where that's ended up.

Bob Bass never sought my input before the trade deadline. My expertise in that area, as the dad of an 11 year old, resides solely in Pokemon cards. I think I can safely say the question of the value of a Pik-a-chu versus a foil Charazard is on Bob's back burner.

I've never choreographed a HoneyBee routine or acted as their wardrobe, make-up, music or hair consultant. Haven't been called on to line up the halftime act. And I don't know why particular players do . . . or don't do . . . anything. David Wesley is really the only guy on the team who acknowledges my existence. Derrick Coleman did glare at me once after I suffered a severe case of mind fog and called him Elden Campbell three times.

In spite of this, when people find out I do PA for the Hornets, I am beset with queries on all aspects of the team. Sorry, folks. I don't know. It's kinda like someone asking the guy at Office Max who sold them their laptop, "What's that Bill Gates fellah *really* up to?"

If anyone at the Hornets wants my suggestions, I'd be more than happy to oblige. In fact, the next time I see Ray, I'll offer my services. When he goes before the city council, I'll be there to yell, "Heeeeeere comes your presentation!"

It's the least I could do.

Science 101 Quiz

Originally published September 17, 1999
© Charlotte Business Journal. All rights reserved.
Reprinted with permission

OK, boys and girls. Time for our annual science quiz. It's still true/false, but I'm tossing in a few multiple choice just to keep you on your toes. I hope you did the assigned reading. Close the books and log off the Web. You have one hour. And remember, as always, no wagering.

1. Mozart makes a great baby sitter.

True – at least that's what the company Neurosmith is banking on. They've developed an electronic box that allows budding Amadeus's (Amadeii?) to create songs by moving blocks with musical phrases stored on them, stimulating their young minds. Hopefully, it won't make your kids too brainy. Then they'd just re-program the blocks to play the Barney theme or old Stones' jams.

2. Bicycles now come with automatic transmissions.

True. The new Autostream by GT Bikes has an electronic shifter that gauges the proper gear based on the speed of the bike. Resist the urge to opt for the leather interior and moon roof.

3. First multiple choice. Einstein was smarter than everyone else because:
a) his brain was bigger
b) his hair was bigger
c) the Zurich school board got that $375 million bond issue passed.

Answer: a) of course. The June 19th issue of Lancet reports a team at McMaster University (where Al's pickled thinker was left) discovered Einstein's brain was not only bigger, it was 15% wider. Wouldn't that make a great Pontiac commercial – "Wider *is* better in Firebirds and parietal lobes." If you answered "B", that would have meant his barber was smarter and C – well, everybody knows how that vote went.

4. April showers bring May flowers.
True – and Mayflowers bring pilgrims, yeah, OK. But it was the only way I could sneak in another new invention, the lighted umbrella. Gallery 2000 has a bumbershoot with a center post that lights up when you twist the handle, ostensibly so you can see and be seen on rainy days. Hey, it could act as the low beams for your automatic transmission bike! What a great gift combo!

5. Second multiple choice - The average temperature in cosmic microwave background radiation is:
a) 2.7 kelvins
b) 6.3 kelvins and hobbes
c) 5.5 melvins
Answer: a) Got to throw a bone to all the cosmologists who read the Business Journal.
b) is a defunct comic strip and
c) is the first attempt at cloning lead singers for the Blue Notes.

6. Ladies, you accepted the date with the wimp because it was the wrong time of the month.
True. According to a study in *Nature*, women, at the highest conception point of their menstrual cycle choose a "masculinized" look for short term relationships, verses a more feminine face during other points; i.e. – a healthy, square-jawed look vs. an open, positive personality look. That's why, on your last date, the guy was rummaging through your purse looking for the Midol. "I can't understand it. That line about having a bike with an automatic transmission used to work every time."
Pencils down. Grades will be posted on my door on Monday.

"Reykjavik, We Have a Problem . . ."

Originally published January 21, 2000
© Charlotte Business Journal. All rights reserved.
Reprinted with permission

So, here we are, two-plus weeks into Y2K. The power's still on. The planes haven't dropped from the sky and Peter, Paul and Mary haven't put out their rap version of Puff the Magic Dragon. All is right with the world.

Unless you're building a road in Hafnarfjordur.

Hafnarfjordur is a town in Iceland, which may be the one reason you sound like you're sneezing when you say the name. Located just south of the capital of Reykjavik, highway engineers there have had to re-route roadways recently due to elves.

Not just elves. There are gnomes, trolls, something called hulafolk and light-fairies, which, of course, are fairies with half the calories of the regular variety.

And it's not just roads that are held up by the Icelandic spirit world. Houses, offices or anything requiring digging are possible targets for the "hidden folk".

Building anything in Iceland has its share of problems in the visible spectrum.

It's hard digging. The island was born of volcanoes; lava is not one of the easiest rocks to bulldoze.

It's cold. Sitting a mere 180 miles south of the Arctic Circle, you can freeze your drill bit in a nanosecond.

But I imagine taking on a reindeer with an attitude would be preferable to going one-on-one with a lava troll.

The problem is all these faerie folk live in the rocks, under the ground and in boulders. (There aren't many trees to speak of, so the radical wood-nymph cabal isn't a factor.) When you dynamite a rock to make way for a road, there's a strong possibility you've just blown up one of the more fashionable gnome condos.

No gnome I know would take that lying down. No, the spirits retaliate by trashing equipment, causing medical mishaps for workers and making other elfish mischief to halt the project.

In America, this would not happen. The legal fees from contractors suing the elves would bankrupt them and they'd have to leave their rock houses and go work making crackers for Keebler. Or worse, local city councils voting for developers would re-zone their boulders and they'd have 30 days to sell and move out.

Not so in Iceland.

According to a story in the Boston Globe, more than 50% of the island nation's 273,000 people think it's probable that the wee people exist. Ten percent are certain of it.

So, rather than have a possible 30,000 irate elf backers picketing the job site, highway officials opt to build around any stones of contention.

After each re-routing, legend says there is a huge spirit party where all the faerie folk get drunk and sing songs like *Troll Out the Barrel* and *There's No Place Like Gnome*.

None of this has affected Iceland's economy. The country revels in high tech and points proudly to a 100% literacy rate.

And the elves keep folks like Bryjolfur Snorrason busy. He's a folklorist who does consulting work for construction firms, pointing out potential problems with the spirit world.

Imagine being the go-between for elves and road crews. Now that's a job for the 21st century.

The Russians and Ronald McDonald

Originally published November 24, 2000
© Charlotte Business Journal. All rights reserved.
Reprinted with permission

Sometimes there's just too much to write about.

Tying together the Teletubbies and the Mir space station. The Catholic Church and Big Macs. Czechoslovakia and rap music.

Who ya gonna call?

There's good news and bad news out of Moscow. The bad news is the Russian version of NASA has made a hard choice concerning the venerable Mir space station. After decades of floating above Mother Earth and Mother Russia they've decided to bring the mother down. Yuri Koptev, spokes-comrade for the Russian Space Agency, announced the decision last week, saying, "Nothing lasts for eternity." Calling the craft "corroding" and "unstable" Yuri also dashed the dreams of American Dennis Tito, who, having more money than the all the people of Uzbekistan and Kazakhstan combined, had already pumped close to $1 million is training to be the first space tourist to visit Mir.

The good news is while Mir is plunging into the ocean off Australia's coast, Russian preschoolers won't be traumatized by the demise of this former Soviet icon. They'll be comfortably ensconced in front their TVs watching the Teletubbies. The BBC announced a deal with RTR (I think RTR is PBS in the Cyrillic alphabet) to air the colorful quartet. That brings the Tubbies country count to 120 and their merchandising to £32 million annually. Perhaps if Mr. Tito would pump another million into the BBC he could be Tinky Winky for a week. And he wouldn't have to worry about Jerry Falwell.

Some yin and yang in the world of fast food as well. The European arm of the McDonald's corporation unveiled plans to build Golden Arches hotels. They'll be upscale, of course, aimed at the business traveler with rooms running up to $200 a night. High speed internet connections will be available in each room along with other business amenities including, I imagine, Ronald McDonald cookies on your pillow each night and a conscientious sommelier who will suggest the right merlot to go with your McNuggets. The bad news? In Rome, Roman Catholic priest Rev. Massimo Salani has condemned fast food. Saying that fast food "too Protestant", Rev. Salani has basically consigned the Happy Meal to perdition. The solution for peace here is obvious. For every hotel they put up, McDonald's builds a place of worship; a McMonastary, if you will. Imagine the opportunity for the abbot, upon greeting guests and pilgrims, being allowed to say, "You want friars with that?"

And finally, just in case you missed it, the number one rap song in Czechoslovakia this week is "Who Let The Pragues Out."

Not really, but it was too good a pun to pass up.

The Envelope, Please

Originally published October 28th, 1998
© Charlotte Business Journal. All rights reserved.
Reprinted with permission

The country is teetering on the brink of political collapse. The stock markets resemble a nervous elevator that forgot to take its Prozac. Wars, floods and famine wrack this fragile globe we lovingly call (unless you're running for Congress in which case you can move so you'll be in the right district) home. So what do we need to ease our worldwide pain? A new charismatic and powerful leader? The true return of Family Values? A wonder drug that allows us to see the good in trial lawyers *and* hog farmers? Nope . . .

We need another award.

OK, so maybe the airwaves are choked with statuette-starved celebrities vying for something other than their million dollar paydays to prove people like them, really like them. What about the common, everyday, tuna-on-whole-wheat guy and gal? The stars get so many choices. You've got your Oscars, your Golden Globes, your People's Choice, your Tonys, Emmys, Happys, Sleepys and Grumpys. What more could there be? The Dopeys would be, if anything, redundant. No, fair citizens. I propose a new award that can be handed out by anyone, to anyone at any time. You would, however, have to ask permission and pay me an exorbitant entry fee for the use of my copyrighted award. Hey, if Michael Jackson can own "Happy Birthday to You" and Phil Jackson can patent "Three-peat" . . . but I digress.

I call my new award – drum roll, please – the NAWUTH!

Relax, friendly Yankee transplants. This is not an antebellum phonetic spelling of the area above the Mason-Dixon Line. It is an acronym and pronounced "nay-wuth".

Picture this, *sil vous plait*. The Nawuth award will be a simple, humble statue cast of the purest available lead and painted with the finest spray paint your entry fee can buy. It will depict a person of indeterminate sex stumbling from atop a gently sloping pedestal. Little gold X's (in the finest cartoon tradition) are engraved where the eyes should be and a golden replica of a length of two-by-four will be connected to the back of the cranium, thus symbolizing the name of the award: Needs A Whack Upside The Head.

The coveted Nawuth would be presented to individuals, businesses, governments, even entire countries for outstanding examples of pig-, bone-, butt- and hard-headedness; in short, occasions for which someone has said of the nominated entity, "Boy, they sure need a whack upside the head!" For the national presentation, it'll be a four hour network special event with Billy Crystal and Whoopie Goldberg slugging it out to see who gets to host. Local awards can be ordered from the NAWUTH Hotline (1-800-WHACK-EM) for only $24.95, plus shipping & handling. We'll have two hours on the Cable Couch Potato Buying Channel with surprise celebrity Whackers.

Some early nominees:

- The entire executive and legislative branches of our federal government. Whack! The former for being so incredibly stupid and inept and the latter for wasting their time and our money on a tale from daytime TV's slush pile.

- NBA owners and players. Whack 'em all! The next one from either side of the table who says, "It isn't about money" gets traded to Barcelona as a ball boy. Wait 'til they see the demands of the powerful Public Address Announcers Union.

- Anyone who gripes about traffic. Whack! More people live here. They drive. Hello? It isn't the light sequence, it isn't an influx of non-Southerners, it isn't El Niño. Leave sooner. Obey the laws. Drive nicer.

Aaah. See how cathartic just nominating someone for a NAWUTH can be? Now all I need is a sponsor. Lowe's or Home Depot, perhaps?

Please send your nominations to me, care of this paper, along with your entry fee. Amounts requiring commas are compulsory.

Letter to Santa v.1999

Originally published December 24, 1999
© Charlotte Business Journal. All rights reserved.
Reprinted with permission

Dear Santa,

Time for my annual letter. I hope this finds you healthy, happy and free of any criminal or civil suits. But since you're not a part of any professional sports team that's a pretty safe bet. Here's my Christmas Wish List:

1. My own line of Y2K designer clothes and accessories. T-shirts, jeans, backpacks; everything from socks to key chains. I've already got the logo: TM?NY!

It's for all of us who know that January 1, 2000 is not the beginning of the new millennium and stands for "The Millennium? Not Yet!" You might not think it ranks up there with *No Fear* or *FUBU* because it's short-lived. But I plan on selling the franchise rights to whoever wants 'em like, say, Rudy Giuliani for his battle royal with Hillary – "The Mayor? New York!" Or maybe the folks fighting the expansion of SouthPark would buy it – "The Mall? No Yielding!" Or perhaps the Lincoln County Commissioners who are trying to ban zoos – "The Mission? No Yaks!" The possibilities are endless. I'll even let you in on the IPO.

2. A working anti-gravity device large enough for my house. I want to float my humble abode to get it out of Mecklenburg County long enough to see what the City Council and County Commission are hatching tax-wise. I don't know what's worse; a bunch of Republicans who pucker up for any developer who comes their way or a bunch of Democrats whose vocabulary is limited to "property tax".

3. An agent. I finished the book, but I'm 0 for 5 in finding an agent. I'll probably end up trying a direct contact to some paperback publisher working out of the Dry Tortugas. Or the Wet Tortugas. Or the Merely Moist Tortugas.

That's about it for the "I Wants". Once again, however, this year I need to clue you in on what I *don't* want to find lurking beneath the tree.

A twelve pack of Bush Water. Yeah, Dubya is selling bottled water on his website. I don't know why. According to an article in The American Prospect, for a buck-fifty a bottle, you can slurp a salute to the Texas Governor who wants to be your president. Considering the EPA thinks Texas is one of top water polluters, you might think twice about drinking it . . . oops! Never mind. It's bottled in Kentucky. Does this mean his running mate will have to offer bourbon on his website?

A painted silver dollar. Who comes up with this stuff? You've seen them in the magazines and on the shopping channels; a Walking Liberty dollar where Ms. Liberty has been decked out head to toe in red, white and blue. All she needs is a cartoon balloon over her head that says, "Hey, sailor. New in town?" I suppose there are some folks who really want to pay $40.00 for an acrylic-laden 1999 dollar. They're the ones P.T. Barnum loved to see coming through the tent flap.

And finally, Santa, three words: no more Pokémon.

Thanks. And here's hoping Rudolph's nose is Y2K compliant.

In a New York Minute

Originally published February 25, 2000
© Charlotte Business Journal. All rights reserved.
Reprinted with permission

You've probably heard the expression, " . . . in a New York minute." No, it's not how long it will take Hillary to dump Bill if she wins the Senate seat. It's a simple, concise connotative phrase giving credit to the Big Apple for having a fast-paced lifestyle. You may be asking yourself, how can this be tied to Czechoslovakian snack foods? And how can it possibly be worthy of space in a business publication? Darn good questions. Read on and be dazzled.

If a New York minute is the epitome of a short amount of time, what could suggest a long one? Popular sentiment attributes slowness of life to those of us in the South. So, a long time would equal " . . . in a Mississippi minute"? " . . . in an Alabama happy hour"? ". . . in a North Carolina legislative session"?

Surely, New York can't have all the good analogies wrapped up. What about other superlatives? Cold. Hot. Tall. Deep. It's doubtful any of those mentioned will catch on with the popularity of the expression from Rudy Guliani's precinct, but considering the free press it would reap, states should be battling for peppy metaphorical phrases like starving terriers over a pork chop. Some suggestions:

Is that martini dry? As an Arizona sandbox.
Can you freeze in South Dakota? In a Minot minute.
How shaky is that AOL/Time-Warner merger? As Hawaiian hula hips.

I was trying to find what other superlatives might be claimed by states by surfing the web and ran across a site called The Brunching Shuttlecocks (www.brunching.com). It popped up after using "ratings" as a search word and leads us to the Eastern European crunchies.

The Brunching Shuttlecocks – as far as I can tell – is a site dedicated to satire. As part of their mission, they rate things. Anything. Lawn ornaments. Greek gods. Marsupials. And Czechoslovakian snack foods. (Just in case you're interested, in the marsupial category the Australian wombat got an A+ rating while the opossum, the only marsupial indigenous to the United States garnered a measly C-. Humph. Those Aussies get the summer Olympics and think they own the world. But, hey! They've got wombats, kangaroos and Tasmanian devils. They've had more *practice* at marsupials than we have . . . but I digress.)

If you think you'll be in the Prague Harris-Teeter any time soon suffering from a serious snack jones, it would behoove you to check out Brunching Shuttlecocks. They'd recommend the Funkys (a B rating), but steer you away from the Krupke Arasikovie (C-) and advise you to avoid the Telka Cha Cha's (D-).

But while the site is very entertaining and the caveat in regard to Telka Cha Cha's is both timely and important, there was nothing to help answer my question about state superlatives. And that's the business tie-in. Come up with a web site that matches states with superlatives and your company would suck in venture capital that would make Red Hat look like a sidewalk lemonade stand. Trust me.

And should anybody ask, "If you were attacked by a Czechoslovakian wombat, would you sacrifice your Telka Cha Cha's to get away?", tell 'em, "In a Minot minute."

I Love a Parade

Originally published November 30, 1998
© Charlotte Business Journal. All rights reserved.
Reprinted with permission

The heady swirl of autumn leaves can only mean one thing: the gutter cleaning man can make his Lexus payment! That, and it's Parade Time in the Carolinas.

This has been a big year for parades. The Annual Carrousel Parade caps off a calendar chock full of brass bands, festive floats and overtime for sanitation workers. There was one weekend in May that saw Uptown streets closed to traffic due to a parade trifecta: the Dragon Boat Festival, the Santacruzan Parade and the March for Jesus.

And as sure as you're certain that the lovely Miss Leaf Mold was waving at *you* from the back of her convertible, you know there are several other upcoming parades you might want to put on your calendar.

Dec.13th - In the wake of the popular Santacruzan Parade, the Jack-o-lanterncruzan and Easterbunnycruzan Parades will take place. Police will allow the parades as long as they aren't cruzan through Hornets' Nest Park.

Jan. 20th - Uptown streets will be closed due to the County Commissioners Parade. The Bill James float will, of course, drive on the right hand side of the street. The Helms/Scher/Carney floats will stay to the left and the Joel Carter, Hoyle Martin and Tom Bush floats won't appear since their wheels fell off.

Feb. 7th - Local arts and theater groups will ride in convertibles down Tryon *and* Trade Streets at the same time with members waving to the crowd. At the Square, the drivers of all 27 cars will hit their accelerators, culminating in a fiery crash, figuring that's the only way they'll get coverage on local TV news programs.

March 21st - The Square will be blocked off for an hour today while Councilman Al Rousso parades around yelling, "I want the clock to go *here!*" An extra hour will be allowed if he decides to call 911.

April 18th - Trade and Tryon Streets will be closed today with four different religious parades. At 11:00 the Baptists will march from Morehead north on Tryon. At the same time the Buddhists will march south from Seventh Street. A Lutheran group will head east from Poplar and a group from Temple Beth El with head west from Brevard. Parade organizers hope that if they get up enough speed, when they hit at the Square they'll meld into a bunch of Unitarians.

May 29th - Uptown streets will be open. Charlotte's first ticker tape parade was canceled due to impending danger to people on the street. Organizers learned that, since ticker tape is no longer used, some of the less intelligent stock brokers planned to toss their computer monitors. The problem was exacerbated when it was discovered the same brokers didn't know most uptown office windows don't open.

June 12th - Uptown streets will be closed today as all 37 local radio stations participate in a parade to salute their uniqueness and commitment to the community. Both owners of the stations declined to be Grand Marshall as they had plans at their homes in New York City and Los Angeles.

July 29th - The school board announced today they will request a $6.3 million bond package be approved to fund a School Parade. Nothing but the finest materials will be used to build the floats. However, they are asking that students, teachers and parents hold bake sales to raise the money for the parade permit itself.

August 19th - The Committee to Stop Road Rage decided to cancel their parade scheduled for today after some difficulty during line-up. One marching band passed another and then slowed down. The ensuing altercation resulted in 35 fistfights, 26 rude gestures and half a dozen sousaphone-benders. Police are on the scene. So are eight television news trucks.

Sept. 3rd - Uptown streets will be closed, not by a parade, but by developers who got approval from city council to re-zone the streets to multi-family. 27,000 new one-bedroom town homes (average price - $375,000) will be built in a five-block area surrounding the Square. Developers say there is no cause for concern. They will put in sidewalks.

Predictions for the New Year 2001

Unpublished

In the tradition of such fine journalistic endeavors as the World Weekly News, the National Enquirer and Vinnie the Shiv's Off Track Tip Rag, I proudly present (small fanfare, please) **_Flynn's Fearless Predictions for 2001_**!

THE INTERNET WILL GROW!
Literally. Through a miscalculation, IT engineers at Red Hat will mistakenly combine a new beta version of Linux with a Chia Pet left over from the office Secret Santa party. The result is an incredible increase in online access speeds, but your desk will look like the outfield wall at Wrigley Field.

ALAN GREENSPAN IS REALLY ELVIS
Not the most shocking revelation, but important when, after legally changing his name to Alan Greenspressley, he ties any reduction of the prime rate to the demand for all of the CEOs of the Fortune 500 companies to perform a doo-wop rendition of "Love Me Tender" at the next WTO meeting.

UPTOWN ARENA VOTE QUESTIONED
The referendum on the new arena reaches an impasse when the tally shows 50% for and 50% against. Both sides lobby to get Katherine Harris to handle the recount for them.

AIRLINE MERGER FALLS THROUGH
The Federal Trade Commission (after consulting hundreds of business leaders, dozens of congressional hacks, eight Ouija boards and FTC Chairman Pitofsky's lawn dart game) will nix the proposed United/U.S. Airways

consolidation. However, minutes later they will approve the creation of United TimeWarner-AOL Airways. Sony Airlines immediately files suit.

PRESIDENT BUSH CLAIMS <u>HE</u> IS ELVIS
First meeting with the Fed chairman is less that cordial.

STOCK MARKET CONTINUES ITS DECLINE
The Dow, NYSE and NASDAQ all linger at end-of-the-year marks in spite of efforts by Alan Greenspressley to prime the economic pump. The prime reaches 6 ½% by mid-July, but inflation continues its inexplicable upward spiral. In a desperate move, Alan calls Red Hat and asks if he can borrow their Chia Pet.

INDEPENDENCE BLVD. PROJECT HALTED
Construction to turn Independence Boulevard into an expressway up to Albemarle Road is shut down after the first day of labor results in a forty foot cinder block wall straddling all lanes at Eastway Drive. Investigation reveals that, during an unfortunate incident at the Planning office involving a whispered suggestion and a cup of hot coffee, the plans for the expressway and the new uptown arena were switched. City D.O.T. officials aren't concerned since any work on the road will probably be torn up again anyway.

BASKETBALL OFFICIALS QUESTION D.O.T.'S DECISION
Representatives for the Hornets want the city to take a closer look at building the new arena in the middle of Independence Blvd. Besides giving new meaning to the phrase "driving the lane", the location would guarantee traffic and the option for luxury sky boxes/toll booths is attractive.

ELVIS RETURNS
And claims he's Al Gore. Demands a recount and a jelly donut.

Peanut Airlines

Originally published September 21, 1998
© Charlotte Business Journal. All rights reserved.
Reprinted with permission

News Item – A federal government agency has mandated that airlines provide "peanut-free" areas on commercial flights taking into consideration people who are allergic to peanuts.

"Hi, there! Welcome to GlobeSpin Air. What is your destination today?"
"Waukegan."
"One to Waukegan. Checking any bags?"
"Yes, checking one bag."
"Sir, FAA regulations require I ask you if you accepted any packages from strangers in the terminal today."
"No, I did not."
"Very, good, sir. Now, are you member of our Often Airborne Club?"
"No."
"Would you like to join? You get 50,000 bonus miles just for standing in line."
"Thanks, no."
"OK! Now, that's round trip to Waukegan with a three hour layover in Fargo, business class. Would you like an aisle or window seat?
"Window, please."
"West or east side of the plane?"
"You can choose that now?"
"Of course, sir. At GlobeSpin Air, we know how important it is to keep the business traveler happy, so we make every accommodation for the..."
"Fine. West side, please."
"And you don't have to sing 'Maria', sir."
"Excuse me?"
"A little airline counter humor, sir. West Side. Maria."
"Oh. I see. Ha-ha."

"You can be a Shark on our Jet!"

"I get it. Thank you."

"Now, will that be peanut or non-peanut?"

"Beg pardon?"

"Would you prefer a peanut or non-peanut section of the plane? Due to happy business travelers that are allergic to peanuts, regulations require us to ask, so will that be peanut or non-peanut?"

"Look, I'm sure that peanut allergies can be very serious, but less than one tenth of one percent of the population has an even mild reaction to peanuts."

"That may be, sir. But it is mandated by regulations that we go through a checklist of possible allergens to make sure you're a happy business traveler. So, peanut or non-peanut?"

"Peanut is fine."

"Cashew or non-cashew?"

"Cashew."

"Almond or . . . "

"Just stick me in with the mixed nuts, OK?"

"OK! Now, I have to ask, sir . . . did you accept any peanuts from any strangers in the terminal?

No, but I am smuggling a bag of caramel corn in my laptop."

"Oh, very good, sir! Your own counter humor! Now, would you prefer natural fibers or synthetics?"

"Is this really necessary?"

"Regulations, sir."

"Of course. Uh . . . natural fibers, then."

"Excellent choice, sir. Mmmm . . . is that Brut you're wearing?"

"No . . . it's English Leather. Why?"

"I love English Leather, but you'll have to stop by the steam room before the final boarding call, sir."

"Steam room?!"

"Federal regulation #542, section 12, sub-section A, paragraph iii - 'No person shall board a commercial flight utilizing a fragrance, odor or dural musk.'"

"Dural musk?"

"We here at GlobeSpin Air, while keeping the business traveler happy, also have to deal with keeping the federal government off our backs and... oh, my, look at the time. I don't think you'll have time to make it to the steam room, sir. I am authorized to wipe you down with this moist towelette . . ."

"No! Isn't there something else you could suggest?"

"Well, GlobeSpin Air engineers tried to come up with a way for happy business travelers to roll down their windows, but at 37,000 feet it was somewhat detrimental to cabin comfort."

"Uh-huh..."

"And we toyed briefly with the idea of spraying aviation fuel on each passenger so they'd all smell like the pilots, but that didn't... well, fly. Hee-hee! More counter humor, sir. Uh, sir... where are you taking your bag? Your flight boards in 15 minutes."

"Changed my mind. I'm walking."

"Walking to Waukegan. How clever, sir. Sir? Would you like to join GlobeSpin's Frequent Walkers' Program? Sir..?"

Does Your Sign Have a Cork In It?

Originally published October 15, 1999
© Charlotte Business Journal. All rights reserved.
Reprinted with permission

Bonjour, mon ami! So, vous are about to travel to *le Europe* (translated "the old world") and see *les views* (the sights), buy *les souvenirs* (the tourist trap junk) and partake in *le cuisine* (food that is banned in every other country.)

Yes, the continent has had a hard time recently with its comestibles. First it was Mad Cow, a blight that saw Ronald McDonald panhandling on street corners wearing a sign that said "Will clown for McMoney". Next, there was a cheese scare in Luxembourg, a bad Coca-Cola crisis in Belgium and for all we know, some kraut that really *was* sour in Germany. Plus, now, they're all in a snit about genetically enhanced foods imported from America.

So, what do valiant Europeans do when every forkful could contain certain gastro-intestinal distress and they're having to run DNA tests on their asparagus?

Drink.

Heavily.

Or . . . come up with a new way to market what they drink. (See? Sooner or later these columns have *something* to do with business.) Yes, those wonderful vintners of Versailles, those intrepid Traipsers of the Grape have decided the best way to grow the stuff that becomes the bubbly is to use the stars.

Astrology, meet the winery. As reported in Business Week, some of the premier French winemakers are now planting, growing and pressing according to age-old formulas backed up with New Age jargon. For those of you schooled in fine wines, the names Domaine Leflaive, Nicholas Joly and Michel Chapoutier mean the top of the vintners' craft. To everyone else they're three guys who helped make Jerry Lewis who he is today. But, in fact, they represent the hottest vine regions – Burgundy and the Loire and Rhone Valleys respectively – and have adopted this astrological approach.

What are the key elements to making Star Wine? First, it is important to supply your grapes with the proper "life forces." Since most grapes are incapable of calling Dionne Warwick, this is accomplished by fertilizing them with – a mild warning to those weak of stomach – a concoction of cow manure mixed with water into a substance called "vortex". This produces a heady little wine, full bodied, yet precocious with a hint of cow. Hmm . . . (sip, sip) must be a Taurus. I shudder to think what they must use to produce a good Capricorn.

Of course after the little vins-to-be are ripe, they are harvested according to precise astrological charts.

Vintner – "Should we harvest, Madam Mephisto?"

M.M. – "Let me peer into my crystal grape . . ."

There is no hard data yet on sales of the celestial vintages, but supposedly the wines of M. Leflaive, M. Joly and M. Chapoutier have come out of crucial wine tastings smelling like – excuse me – having the fine bouquet of a rosé.

You've been alerted. The next time you're at The Lamplighter or La Bibliotheque and the sommelier asks for your sign, don't tell him to stick a cork in it. Request the astral wine chart. Then go with the Pisces chardonnay. It's not very dry, but it won't leave you with the stinging hangover of the Scorpio Chablis.

License Plate, Thy Name is Vanity

Originally published August 18, 2000
© Charlotte Business Journal. All rights reserved.
Reprinted with permission

Vanity plate.

The phrase used to conjure up such distasteful images, the same way *"raw sewage"*, *"tax return"* and *"political candidate"* still do. That is, until I broke down and got one.

Think of the challenge: summing up your life in a mere eight blue typographical characters; saying something that illuminates your religious convictions, the pride in your profession, the very essence of your being. Or that you got drunk at a frat party and from that moment on everyone referred to you as BOOPER.

Of the 6.8 million license plates piloting around the Old North State, some 200,000 are of the vanity variety. They cost an extra $20 a year. Imagine that. Your fellow Tar Heels forking over an extra $4 million a year to give you the pleasure of sitting at a stoplight trying to figure out what FLYTEQ4 stands for. That's an actual plate I stumbled upon on WRAL-TV's web site. The site has an access to the vanity plate data base where you can look up any combination of symbols on issued plates. While trying to decide what to use in my allotted spaces, I poked around the ones that would normally be associated with me. There are 75 permutations of JAMES. Boring. Why be just another First in Flight JAMES?

Looking in the section from FLEA2 to FLOORS2U, there's only one FLYNN and it's FLYNN#3. (Makes you wonder what happened to #'s 1 and 2.) The only others close to my surname are FLY-BY-U, FLYBABIE and the aforementioned FLYTEQ4. Still, using one's name or a derivative of it seems so narcissistically gauche. I looked at examples that used punctuation marks as starters. The standout was !?#X*!. With the rather stringent rules on what is and isn't allowed to be stamped, I didn't think you could say that on a license plate, but with a Democrat in the White House for so long things have obviously gotten lax.

The neatest thing about the site (www.wral-tv.com/5newfocus) is a gadget called the Plate-o-Matic. You can stamp your very own North Carolina license plate with whatever you want on it. No, you can't print it out and put it on your Lexus, but you can e-mail it to a buddy and tell him or her just how you feel through a license plate. And I might cautiously add there are no language restrictions for *these* plates. If you could e-mail anonymously, wouldn't it be fun to send EASLY4ME to the Vinroot headquarters? (Yeah, I left the "E" outta Easley. I've only got eight spaces, for cryin' out loud.)

Back to my plate. It's AYORT. Figure that one out, plate aficionados. The first correct answer gets a pair of tickets to the Hornet's home opener. Send your guesses to me care of this paper. People whom I've already told are not eligible.

Good luck. And remember, when trying to figure out a vanity plate while you're driving, put down the cell phone, the newspaper, the lipstick and the coffee cup first.

The Web's Ten Worst Sites

Originally published August 27, 1999
© Charlotte Business Journal. All rights reserved.
Reprinted with permission

So, like, are you a web surfer, dude?

According to the covers of most of the national print media, we all are . . . whether we have a computer or not. Five of the mags I subscribe to have recently focused on "The Ten Best (insert your demographic here) Web Sites." Popular Science has the best science web sites. Business Week has the top business URLs. Newsweek and Time both have boxes dedicated to the hot computational destination of the week. Some of the sites can give you information that is quite valuable, including links to other pages of related topics. I got great information for the cracker column I wrote several months back from the Nabisco and Keebler web pages.

Some sites, I'm convinced, are the nefarious fronts for various servers (the guys you have to go through to access the web) and get a kickback for the amount of time – and money – spent on being on line with them; example – gambino.com. It's fun, but you can get sucked into squandering hours, staring and clicking until you're glassy-eyed and drooling, having racked up an $87.00 charge on AOL or Mindspring. Consider yourself warned.

And there are a number of places to go for freeware and shareware that offer you software at little or no cost that can, when installed properly, allows your machine to do myriad wonders, like letting your A: drive double as a pastry oven.

Surfing the web is kind of like trying to read all the books in the library. There's almost too much information. So, I guess it's helpful, nay, a public service for the national media to take the full stalk of their areas of interest, toss them into the online trade winds, separating the www.wheat from the computer chaff.

But that overblown metaphor is, as they say, only half the story.

Here are the top ten worst web sites:

10. A site that, if you log on, starts sending you junk e-mail from Dr. Seuss - www.greeneggsandspam.com.

9. Page with nothing but a picture of six female sheep - www.DoubleEweDoubleEweDoubleEwe.com. (It's hard enough to read and harder to type.)

8. URL featuring the first Rastafarian motorcycle company - www.marleydavidson.com.

7. A search engine that will only find stuff in Indiana - www.yahoosier.com.

6. A page offering for sale all-wool sweaters with a picture of George Bush, Jr on the front - www.DoubleEweDubya . . . ok, no more sheep gags.

5. An updated conspiracy site offering proof that the music of the Fab Four can destroy trees - www.pinebarkBeatles.com.

4. URL placed on the web by the City of New York welcoming Hillary Rodham Clinton to town - www.Here'sYerVillageRightHere!.com.

3. Site offering self-help books to cattle farmers who've had to sell off their stock due to the drought - www.barnsandnobull.com.

2. Another conspiracy site promoting the idea that Bill Gates is trying to take over the world - www.WeAreMicrosoftResistanceIsFutileB.org. (B.org. Borg. Not a Star Trek fan, huh? Oh well . . .)

1. A site featuring a huge picture puzzle game dedicated to finding every piece of Germany's infamous former national barrier - www.where'stheberlinwaldo.com.

You'll have to research the rest. And if you use my server, tell 'em I sent you. I get a $10 credit.

One Less Pole Sign

sigh... another unpublished one

This is a true story. The names have been changed to protect the author.

To the owner of the business "Sell Your House in 12 Days!"

I tore down one of your stinkin' signs.

It was tacked oh so professionally to a power pole at the intersection of Sardis and Rama Roads, just below the large YIELD sign. I say professionally because the nail had one of those plastic guards on it so the head wouldn't put too much pressure on the corrugated board and make it bend in the middle. At least that's my theory. I'm not thoroughly acquainted with the physics of cheap advertising devices.

"Professional", too, because your service is presented in such a classy way. It ranks right up there with "Lose 3 Inches of Flab in 24 Hours!" and "Earn $10,000 a Month From Your Recliner!" I can imagine the number of people who flock to a business whose advertisement competes on the same playing field with yard sale announcements on pieces of torn packing boxes and rain-stressed flyers for lost pets. The fact that you are in violation of several city ordinances shouldn't deter you from promoting such an obviously pristine and respectable business.

"What ordinances?", you ask. Why, the ones that prohibit such signs. They're the ones in Section 13 of the city zoning codes. I'm sure you looked them up since I assume you are of a species that has opposable thumbs. You probably observed with special interest the part about signs "that are similar in color, design, and appearance to traffic control signs, vehicular signs as defined in Section 13.102." Hmm . . . your sign is red lettering on a white background. The YIELD sign is . . . ah, but your sign is a *rectangle* and YIELD is a *triangle*. You must have gotten the well-known "Geometry Variance" when posting your sign.

And you placed it snugly beneath the YIELD sign so it was hard to tell where one stopped and the other started. This seamless flow from traffic sign to advertising was probably part of your MBA thesis, but it bothers me. You see, from around 7:00 AM until 8:30AM, some of the drivers who sprint through that particular intersection aren't as alert as they should be. I call them Drivers Of Limited Thinking or DOLTs. They are so concerned with getting to work, eating breakfast, clinching that 7:48 AM deal on their cell phone, putting on make-up or, yes, reading the paper, that they sometimes actually block the crosswalk the kids in the neighborhood (including my 15 year old and 6 year old) use to get to school. Heck, they block the whole intersection and run red lights, too, which I'm pretty sure violates a couple of the more trivial traffic laws.

So, since they're so engrossed in getting to where they're going – and they *are* DOLTs – I figured having one more thing to look at – something that might blend in with a traffic sign – rather than paying attention to children in the crosswalks, could be construed as . . . oh, I don't know . . . dangerous and stupid?

I didn't take all of them down. You thoughtfully plastered four or five more on other poles at the intersection and at varying heights. A chapter from your doctoral dissertation, perhaps? A small footnote for your paper: you'll be happy to know the one I got was recycled that very morning.

I hope losing that one stinkin' sign didn't cause any hardships for you, like having to sell a house in 13 days. You might try putting up another one.

Go ahead. Make my day.

Starquakes!

It's been a tough couple of months, campers. Hurricanes, wars, terrorists, the new line-up on Fox. Not to mention Jake's interception. You getting the feeling, like I am, that Chicken Little was right?

Funny you should mention the sky falling. As if you didn't have enough to worry about (insert scary music here - DUHN, Duhn, duhhhhn!), there's starquakes.

No, I do not speak of a new sugar-slathered part of a balanced breakfast. Yeppers, there's actual quakes in them thar stars. (Good news – Karl Rove talked Dubya out of a helicopter fly-over to survey the damage.)

Granted, the starquake that has astronomers' telescopes in knots is 50,000 light years away, but wait 'til you hear what *might* happen. First some scientific background to lend this opus some legitimacy . . .

How do we know there are such things as starquakes? I'll get to that in a moment. Turn now in your Astronomy 101 textbooks to page 128. Most of you know that stars are giant balls of gaseous material, but enough about Russell Crowe. Let's speak astronomically. There are other stars bouncing around the firmament called neutron stars, made mostly of iron. Their centers contain a thick soup of atomic particles that, combined with their iron crusts, generate magnetic fields trillions of times stronger than Earth's. The strongest of these are called magnatars. They shouldn't be confused with minotaurs – which, of course, are mythical beasts who roam around mazes – or mini-tars, which are itty-bitty British sailors.

The magnatar in question is designated SGR 1806-20. I shall call this huge, round, heavenly body Maggie. (You may insert your own Kirstie Alley joke here.) Scientists have been watching Maggie for years, even though she's kept her shades pulled down and threatened them with restraining orders. Maggie is surrounded by the strongest magnetic field in the known universe, making a starquake pretty much inevitable. This field, along with the right eau de cologne, also makes it easier for her to get a date on the weekends.

Steve Schwartz of the Imperial College in London reports in an interview with Space.com that the starquake caused a three mile long crack in

Maggie's crust, allowing the neutrons, protons and electrons inside to leak out. That radiation leak is what caught the attention of astronomers around the world.

You might think, hey, this is a *star* we're talking about. Maggie's a gal that's been around the block a few times. A three mile crack in her crust is kinda like celestial crow's feet. Some Botox, a little Maybelline and she's ready to party. Unfortunately, Maggie is only six miles in diameter. You don't need an abacus to figure that one out.

Should we be concerned? Heck-fire, no! says Steve Schwartz. This little leak, 50,000 light years away, only blinded a few satellites in orbit and *briefly altered Earth's upper atmosphere.*

Um... Steverino? Altered the atmosphere? *Altered the atmosphere?!?* Don't know about you Imperial College chaps, but that kinda ranks right up there on my personal Pucker Meter.

The report goes on to further reassure an already Zantac-popping population that, had the leak occurred within 10,000 light years of our cute li'l planet, it would have fried the ozone layer. After that, a tube of SPF-8 Billion couldn't stop us from becoming croutons.

Not to worry, though, fellow space travelers. The nearest magnatar is 13,000 light years away. Yessiree-bob. We got us a 3,000 light year buffer zone. Probably only cause a few split ends and the growth of a third nostril. I feel better already.

Still, might be worth a call to my insurance agent to see if she offers neutrino emission coverage.

Funny?

Not so much....

Goodbye, Checkie

Originally published in the Charlotte Observer August 17, 1991

This is an open letter to the person who was on the cash register at the store the other night. To protect the innocent, I won't say which store. Just that it was a major grocery store. Let's call it Dixie Teeter Lo & P Sav-a-Bunch. I also won't say whether this person was male or female, young or old, black or white. I'll just call you Checkie.

Checkie, you lost your store a customer. And not for any of the reasons most people reject a store. You didn't short-change me. You didn't put the bread on the bottom of the bag and drop a can of stewed tomatoes on it; all I bought was a gallon of milk and a Teenage Mutant Ninja Turtle sticker book for my son. You didn't sneer or growl at us, call my mother names or burn an American flag. The problem was you didn't do anything.

You barely acknowledged my presence at your register, even after I said hello. I can't believe you didn't see me, as I was a large, bearded man wearing a Discovery Place dinosaur t-shirt with an excited nine-year-old. You didn't say "hi" or "hello" or "kiss my grits." You chewed your gum, ran the milk and sticker book over your holographic scanner, monotonically announced the total, took my money, gave me my change, sacked up the stuff and moved on to the next customer *without once looking at me!*

OK, it was 9 on a Friday night. To give you the benefit of the doubt, you might have been at the end of a long day or just started what was to be a long night at this 24-hour store. Maybe it was a personal problem: you and your significant other had a spat, the cat's sick, a check bounced. Perhaps you were totally bummed out by this John Sununu mess.

This may sound heartless, but I don't particularly care. I am your customer. And as your customer, I deserve certain things.

I deserve eye contact of some sort. A smile and a hello. And most importantly, I deserve a thank you. A single, sincere one. You should thank me, Checkie. Not for spending $3.48 or $348.00, but for being a quiet, pleasant customer who just helped pay your salary.

There are bastions of friendly service. Ed Tubal has a plaque in each Sonny's restaurant that reminds his employees about the importance of the customer. John Barringer at Little Professor Books has a staff that would sooner die than not be pleasant to a customer. Dean Pennell at the lumber counter at Hechingers on Independence recently went out of his way, while barraged with customers, to help me out. Dean doesn't know me from Adam's housecat, but handled his job with knowledge and humor.

Happily it would take longer to list businesses that are concerned about their customers than those that don't seem to be. But I have run into more than one Checkie.

So, to Checkie, and more importantly to the managers of all the Checkies: take a hint. The customer who leaves angry, no matter how good the product, will never come back.

A Perfect Face for Radio

An American Hero . . . Who Fixes Trucks

Originally published in Mecklenburg Neighbors September 25, 1991

I found a hero the other day. His name is Vic and he drives Ford F-350 diesel tow truck.

The story: My small pickup decided to give up the ghost in the southbound lane of I-85 at the US 29/601 interchange between Concord and Kannapolis. Of course, it died right in the middle of rush hour – and the ubiquitous construction had traffic down to one lane and drivers were wishing they could reach half the posted speed limit.

Luckily, my pickup had enough oomph to mosey into the breakdown lane, where I tried in vain for twenty minutes to get it going again.

I stewed in my own juices and was bathed in the grit from passing autos and tractor-trailers on the mile-and-a-half trek to a pay phone. I patiently explained to the 1-800 lady that there was no I-35 in North Carolina and that Highway 29 and 601 are the same road. She assured me help was on the way. As I cussed and grumbled my way back toward my deceased vehicle, a tow truck with "Vic's Auto Service" on the doors pulled up beside me on the entrance ramp to the interstate.

"You the man with the truck?"

That's how I met Vic Stirewalt.

Vic has his own garage on West Ninth Street in Kannapolis. West Ninth isn't a slum, but it isn't the garden spot of K-Town, either. Vic's garage is a rustic two-room structure surrounded by cars, parts of cars and weeds.

My own prejudices bubbled beneath the surface. Great! I've been saddled with Kannapolis' version of Gomer or Goober.

I couldn't have been more wrong. And my car couldn't have been in better hands.

Make no mistake. Vic is about as good a good ol' boy as they come. But don't confuse him with Doug Marlette's Dub DuBose. He has firm ideas about what's proper and what's not. The TV show "Married. . . With Children" isn't proper.

Based on his itinerary for the past week, he practically lives behind the wheel of his tow truck. He enjoys racin', both watching and participating – he has a couple of dirt track cars in the garage – and he shared one of his prized possessions with me: a picture of Dale Earnhardt and his stock car, signed by Dale and Bill Elliot.

And Vic fixed my truck.

I know as much about auto engines as an orangutan knows about quantum physics. But Vic knows engines. Vic knew what was wrong with mine just by listening to what it was and wasn't doing. The technical explanation: the control module in the distributor wasn't controlling or distributing. Vic's explanation: "You ain't gettin' no fire."

I rode with Vic to the parts store for a new module and we talked. About my former job in radio. About cars. About my lack of knowledge of cars. About his lack of knowledge of radio. Vic said that was no big deal. Nobody could know everything. He didn't want to know how to be a surgeon. "I'd have to be real mad at somebody to cut on 'em," he joked.

Vic sparred verbally with the folks at the parts store over the proper control module. As we walked out, he shook his head. "I was fixin' cars while they was still in dirty diapers."

We went back to the shop; he fixed, we talked as the sun when down and the mosquitoes chewed on us.

OK, so how does this make Vic Stirewalt a hero? First, he was there when I needed him. It was late in the day; he could have closed up, told me to rent a car and come back tomorrow for mine. He fixed it there and then.

Second, he did his work competently and wasn't condescending to me, a mechanical bumpkin.

Third, it was obvious he is a community man. He recognized people and they recognized him with a wave. I can't say for sure, but I'd wager Vic has been in Kannapolis all his life and likes it there.

And finally, he gave me good service for a fair price, which is a diminishing commodity these days.

I think Vic is a pretty good representation of the oft-mentioned American Dream. He's his own boss in a world of conglomerates, doing what he loves to do. He's a good mechanic. I imagine some of the big auto-repair chains would be tickled pink to have someone like Vic working for them. But he seems content to work on West Ninth, drive his tow truck, trade insults with his friend Floyd and enjoy racin'.

If you ever run into car trouble in Kannapolis, want it fixed right and don't demand an air-conditioned waiting room with cable TV, give Vic a call.

He'll be glad to talk to you.

Ad of Infamy

Originally published in the Mecklenburg Neighbors December 29, 1991

I got angry at an ad in a magazine today. And I'm not completely sure why.

Newsweek's issue was about the 50th anniversary of Pearl Harbor. And on page 61 was an ad for "Target Pearl Harbor", the special commemorative edition videotape. But not just any tape. It's "...the whole story! ... gripping footage of the Day of Infamy ... only $19.98 ... great holiday gift!"

"Oh, why not," you say. "It's just another Pearl Harbor piece." Every network had a special on it. Most major magazines, as Newsweek did, devoted entire issues to it. Even this paper did a special series on the attack. Politicians are either embracing it or trying to ignore it, depending on whether they're talking to their constituents or foreign trade concerns. Why should someone producing a video about Pearl Harbor stir my wrath?

Why, indeed.

The attack on Pearl Harbor happened 13 years before I was born. Forty-one years before my first son was born. My father was 19. And Pearl Harbor changed life for all of us.

It was a focal point of my education. World War II could be summed up for me by the words "Pearl Harbor" and "D-Day". I grew up to Glenn Miller more than to Elvis Presley. My knowledge of the European theater was limited to the TV show "Combat" with Rick Jason and Vic Morrow handling things over there. The war in the Pacific took on extra importance because my father was a Marine pilot stationed on Enjibi in the Eniwetok atoll in 1943.

My sisters and I knew Dad was a fighter pilot during the war and marveled in the glamour. His model of his F4U Corsair graced his dresser. We saw the snapshots of his squadron. We giggled at the wings tattooed on his chest. I got to wear his flight jacket and helmet on occasion. I still have a picture of me in kindergarten wearing the goggles, standing next to a crudely drawn picture of a plane crashing; the caption "My Dad was in the War. He shot down 'Japs'" was allowed then, political correctness not being in vogue in 1959.

We all learned to play Acey-Deucy (the Marines version of backgammon) and learned the words to "Oh, Enjibi", sung to the tune of "Oh, Christmas Tree". It was the song the squadron sang over the radio when returning to the field. "Oh, Enjibi" were the only words.

His personal involvement was rarely discussed. In fact, I don't remember being regaled with an overabundance of war stories, bad or good. I do remember listening covertly to conversations Dad had with his fellow fliers at reunions. They weren't "boy, we kicked their butts!" sessions. They spoke of missions. Of seeing planes in their squadron go down. Of who made it to the beach. And who didn't.

It was as though the war was something they didn't want us kids to have to think about. They went to war, they did their duty, fought, saw friends die, were proud of their involvement, but glad it was over. While the conflict was on a global scale, for my father and his compatriots, the war was very personal. I imagine it was that way for all the soldiers, sailors and fliers, men and women, on both sides.

And that's why I think I'm angry about the video. Not that it was made. History needs to be documented and videos can be very effective teaching tools. But the way it's being marketed grates. This ad turns a historical and painful day into some kind of bad TV series.

More from the ad: "Spectacular never-before-seen footage . . . exclusive interviews with survivors . . . from the best-selling book!" There's a toll-free number for your credit card orders. I'm surprised it wasn't 1-800-JAP-BOMB. I sincerely hope the content isn't as sensationalized as the advertisement.

This type of hype trivializes the sacrifices made on Dec. 7, 1941 and the years after that. It bring the observance of the "day that will live in infamy" to the level of huckstering for bamboo steamers and "greatest love song" collections.

I doubt my dad will find this under the tree this Christmas. And I doubt if he'll be disappointed.

Oh, Say . . . Can You Sing?

Originally published in the Charlotte Observer July, 1983

It's that time of year again. The Fourth of July has come and gone, fireworks have slashed the night sky, patriotism has swelled with pride in many an American's bosom and the pundits have started taking pot shots at our national anthem. I've seen no fewer than six articles by columnists countrywide rake up old and forlorn arguments that add up to nothing more than "Banner" bashing. It's an easy thing to do. So, I thought it was time somebody said something nice about F.S. Key's opus.

"The Star Spangled Banner" gets a bum rap mainly because of those of us who sing it. Among the Hornet faithful up in Section 124 last season, the question often was which would last longer, the game (with several mind-numbing losses) or the national anthem?

Allow me to preface this with a couple of things. First, most of the soloists who sang the anthem had gorgeous voices. And, second, I'm as patriotic as the next American. I am one of the few people who defend our national anthem when the perennial debate arises about changing it to the popular (but in my opinion banal) "America the Beautiful". I've sung the "Banner" more than a few times at Hornets games and down at Knights' Castle. I've performed it as a soloist and as part of a chorus.

It's a tough song to sing. It spans two octaves and requires lung power. The lyrics are easy to mess up if you're under pressure. For us amateurs, it takes a large dollop of good ol' American courage to sing it by yourself in front of thousands of rabid sports fans. I take nothing away from anyone who sings the "Banner" solo, whether it is aria quality or a Rosanne clunker.

So, why do some soloists barrage us with their seemingly endless renditions of the "Star Spangled Banner"?

At heart, it is a simple song. It was an old English drinking song before Francis Scott Key set new lyrics to it. And thus it should be sung, by us simple folk at least, simply.

I would not think of casting the aspersion on my fellow game soloists that they are more thrilled with the sound of their own voices than with the anthem. And an occasional variation on the theme can be enjoyable. It's always a treat when Charlotte's Mr. Zerrelli steps to the mike. Who can forget Ben Vereen's rendition that opened the Hornets' season or Whitney Houston's powerful arrangement for the Super Bowl. There is an inherent power and majesty in "The Star Spangled Banner" that speaks to the greatness of this country, more than "America the Beautiful" or "God Bless America" ever will.

Unfortunately, power and majesty occasionally bow to boredom. I clocked some of the soloists last year at Hornets games. A couple have come close to four minutes. At best, "The Star Spangled Banner" should take about two minutes, give or take 15 seconds. Anything more is self-indulgent. The Hornets have put a time limit on the pre-game prayer. Maybe it's time for a shot clock on the "Banner", too.

Some will say it is unfair to put a time limit on patriotism. I say it is unfair for any soloist to upstage our national anthem. It is a song that everyone who is in the arena, park or stadium should be able to sing along with, sharing a common moment of allegiance. Maybe if we soloists would make our renditions more enjoyable . . . and shorter . . . thoughts of changing the national anthem to another tune would become a hollow argument. And we'd happily get to the American ideals of playing ball and eating nachos sooner.

Radio - Where is the Public Service?

Originally published in the Charlotte Observer July 2, 1999

What hath WBT wrought?

The recent "try-out" of an on-air talent and subsequent public backlash of his ill-timed and ill-thought prank makes this former WBT staffer shake his head with wonder and disappointment. It's like being an alumnus of a prestigious university who watches his alma mater become known, not for education, but for keg parties and undergraduates mooning the faculty.

WBT has been a part of the two Carolinas for 77 years. More than half of that time, it has been a major influence on me, both as a listener and an employee. WBT was a fixture in the car when my dad drove us to school. It was the radio Grail for us broadcast students at Appalachian State. And it was the culmination of a dream for me when I joined the staff in 1981.

Why? Because, as one of the first radio stations in America, as the "50,000 watt blowtorch of the Southeast", as the most listened to station in Charlotte, WBT lived up to the ideal that had been drilled into me as a student of radio: serve in the public interest. Serving in the public interest was and is the primary criterion of the FCC for granting a license.

The definition of serving in the public interest has more permutations than Dennis Rodman's hair color. In the last ten years, with deregulation and consolidated ownership, those definitions have expanded exponentially, diluting whatever meaning the phrase once had.

But in 1977, when I entered the Real World of Radio, the interpretation that was my broadcasting benchmark was this: entertain and inform truthfully. Whether you were reading the news or spinning records there were standards and there were limits. When I was on the air did I create characters? Of course. Did I lampoon local, state and federal governments? In a heartbeat, whenever they deserved it. I'd sneak a toe up to the line, too, but I would not intentionally cross it.

Did I ever screw up? You bet. There isn't a radio personality around who could truthfully say that haven't uttered something bone-headed on an open microphone. The numerous stories of on-air faux pas are what keep the conversation lively at reunions. Announcers, in the split second moment of live radio, will make mistakes. A wrong word, an inappropriate comment can lead to reprimands and firings. Two local announcers have been sacked this year for just such occurrences.

In the mid-'80s, the first mention of a death due to Tylenol tampering was made during my show. I tried to make a joke about it coming out of the newscast. I was blasted for it, inside and outside the building – deservedly so – and I apologized on the air. But never during my years on the air did I intentionally lie to the listeners or lead them to believe a piece of creative fluff was news. Anything that was a "bit" was billboarded that way. To do otherwise was unthinkable, not just in regard to my own reputation, but to the reputation of WBT.

The majority of the announcers I worked with shared this mind set. The change in thinking in this regard is unfortunately not restricted to WBT manager Randall Bloomquist and his auditioner. It is endemic to the industry. Radio, competing with everything from its old nemesis TV to the newer threat, the Web, finds itself fighting for audience.

Current programming wisdom believes the easiest way to garner listeners is to sensationalize and shock. Obviously, the management of WBT concurs, approving the latest stunt before it aired and then dismissing it as a practical joke.

The rationale that there's no harm done is as sophomoric as the prank itself. Anyone who doubts the possible damage should look at radio history. Over 60 years ago, Orson Welles and his Mercury Theater of the Air adaptation of "The War of the Worlds" caused a nationwide panic. And that was with disclaimers before, during and after the show.

But, hey. This is the dawn of the 21st century. Surely, in 60 years radio audiences have become hipper, more intelligent, more jaded than the pre-war bucolics frightened by a phony Mars invasion. And if there are bumpkins listening out there who can't take a joke, then they should just "lighten up". It got people talking, right?

Perhaps. But is that a viable excuse for broadcasting misleading information? Is that serving in the public interest? No. When you abuse a public trust, especially one that is inherent in broadcasting, it's tough work to regain it. For the sake of the grand institution that is WBT, I hope Mr. Bloomquist will work a little harder.

Memo to a Sports Critic

Originally published in the Charlotte Observer April 20, 1994

(John Vitti, a writer for the New York Times, wrote an editorial critical of his evening spent at a Charlotte Hornets game. This was my response.)

To: John Vitti
NY Times Syndicate
From: James K. Flynn
Hornets' PA Guy

Dear John,
Jeez, what a sourpuss.
 Did you get aholta (please notice, John, the colorful Southernism "aholta" which we use occasionally during time-outs to rally the bumpkins in the seats... it means "a hold of") a bad hot dog? Maybe since the Knicks are in a slump you were having a bad pencil day. True, they're already playoff bound, but Patrick's had the flu and Starks is out and... I digress.
 Obviously, you have stopped being a fan and become a critic. "Critic" has become a four-letter word in my personal dictionary. Critics today seem to derive the most joy in their work when they can find something bad about everything they see. This is not curmudgeonly well-place retrospect or even knowledgeable pique at a substandard performance. It's just trying to find something nasty to say about the event critiqued and pass it off as deep journalistic introspection. If that's what your job is, you did a good job.
 This is another spin you could have put on the game. You could have said it was a Monday night crowd who had fought Charlotte traffic to fill an

arena for a team other cities would have given up for dead three months ago. You could have found out about the Honeybees choreographer who was in a car wreck the day before and how those lovely young ladies worked up their routines for the game.

Did you not hear the cheers each time the team broke the huddle at the bench and I welcomed them back to the court with "Here come your Hornets!"? Did you not hear the ovation for the "big, fat fan"? We affectionately call him Flipper and he's been a fan favorite for years. But you were so involved in your reportorial angst that you probably didn't talk to him.

You might have come down from your lofty journalistic perch and talked to this "boy who cried" Hornets and seen that he is just as raving a fan as those Hog Hat wearers you seem to idolize. No Hog Hat have I, but a simple baseball cap I got six years ago shooting a TV commercial with Kurt Rambis. On it is a vast assortment of Hornets pins that make it very heavy to wear and can cause grave injury when I smack my forehead over some boneheaded officiating call. And I just washed it for the first time at the beginning of this season. How's that for rabid, eccentric fanaticism, bucko?

You must have been so involved with grinding your personal ax against us poor, bored, deluded hicks (who have only one major league team within hundreds of miles, boo-hoo) that you missed the excitement, color, noise and pure, unabashed joy we have watching the Hornets play ball. And you could also ask the players if they can feel the energy.

Yeah, there's a lot going on. But here's a news flash for you, Mr. Former Assistant Sports Editor: it's show business. I'd explain how show business and a 24-second shot clock go together, but I know you must hurry on to your next riveting assignment – perhaps reveling in the glory of the dead spots in the Boston Garden's floor.

Come back any time, John. But take your time. Meanwhile, stick it in your ear. We won.

Sincerely,
James K. Flynn

"Ol' Hugo Was a 'Messin'…"

Written for 'BT Memories, an on-line nostalgia site for former Jefferson-Pilot folk, wonderfully wrangled by Reno Bailey www.btmemories.com

Radio and Disasters

Anyone who has ever worked in radio and television can speak of defining moments in their careers, whether they were on the air or behind the scenes in engineering, traffic or sales. Get-togethers are always rife with tales of daring-do. For us on-air types, these typically consist of run-ins with management, great interviews, who did what shift when, and that all time favorite, words that should not be said… that were.

We also gauge our life at the microphone from a historical sense. Over the course of 15 or 20 years, news of the turmoil of this country and the world are filtered through us to our listeners and viewers. These events cannot help but leave imprints on announcers, both good and bad. Herb Morrison isn't a name that most people recognize until you tell them he was the guy on the air in 1937 when the Hindenburg went up in flames in Lakehurst, NJ. His engineer that day, Charles Nehlsen, is another name mostly lost to history. But, as it should be, the event has overshadowed the reporters.

I'm sure there are broadcasters who can point to the Kennedy assassinations, and King's, as the focus of their days on air. The dismantling of the Berlin Wall, 9-11 and the World Trade Center and, for me, the Challenger disaster are all moments that can help define a career.

While all these events affect announcers, unless you were directly involved at the location— like Mr. Morrison—there is still an almost necessary detachment that allows us to perform our jobs in a professional manner. It's when the disaster hits home—and we can still deliver the news, service and, yes, entertainment—that we can point with pride at a job well done.

Landfall

Such was the case with Hurricane Hugo. Who knew a hurricane could reach Charlotte? Lots of rain, yes. Probably some wind. But Hugo was still a hurricane when it reached Mecklenburg County in September of 1989.

The power was already out when I got up at 4:00 AM that Friday morning. Usually, I spent a half hour on the computer, checking the news and writing before heading for the station for a 5:30 air time. Since there was no juice to feed my electronic habit, I left early. The rain and the wind were strong, but I had no idea I was driving into work through a hurricane. I could see sparks all along the route from downed power lines. Few tree limbs blocked the road; this was the front side of the storm—or perhaps the eye; the worst was yet to come.

By the time I arrived at 1 Julian Price Place, the engineering staff, along with Tom Desio who was on overnights, were trying to get power to the board. The transmitter had it's own power source, but powering the board required ingenuity. Orange drop cords snaked down the hall, out to generators in the loading dock.

My partner, Don Russell, was already on task as well. Don liked to get to the station early, read the papers and check the wires. With no power, the lights on the phone that told us of incoming calls were dark, so Don, along with everything else, was randomly pushing lines to see who was calling in.

An extremely important part of the morning show, even in good weather, was our Accu-weather guru, Dr. Joe Sobel. We had a limited number of sockets to plug things into, so the piece of equipment that allowed phone calls on the air wasn't a priority. (This was just a few years before the advent of cell phones.) We got Joe on the air by my holding the earpiece of the nighttime producer's phone headset inches away from my microphone. Through occasional bursts of feedback, Joe was on the air.

My most vivid memory of that morning came just after 6:00 AM. One of the landmarks of the building was a large, beautiful old dogwood that graced the patio just outside the Pine Terrace dining room. The strongest winds and rain of the morning were pounding the huge picture windows of the studio. Suddenly, the tree slammed against the window—two stories up—and disappeared into the darkness.

The rest of the day is a blur. Delineation of air shifts disappeared. We stayed on until H. A. Thompson could make it in, and all the announcers came in as needed. Of course, as an air staff, we were used to handling weather emergencies, but mainly on the level of school and business closings for snow. Experience and professionalism paid off. Examples of what could only be classified as heroic measures came to light, the most memorable one being Engineer Bob White's trip to the transmitter site on Nations Ford Road during the height of the storm. Pulling into the parking lot, Hugo's winds toppled the massive Tower A, just missing Bob's car.

The Aftermath

Over the next days and weeks, WBT—and all the radio facilities in the region—stepped up with what the FCC originally sited as a basis for granting licenses: serving in the public interest. Information on everything from directing power crews to where they were needed, to where listeners could find ice made it on air. Everyone at the station—air staff, engineering, sales, promotion, traffic and management—rolled up their sleeves and ignored the clock to keep the station working and serving the public.

Only one of WBT's three towers remained standing. With special dispensation from the FCC, we were allowed to remain on a daytime pattern, so B Tower sent our signal over a wider, localized area.

Television covered the scope of the damage magnificently. But Radio became the cathartic release Charlotte desperately needed. The phone lines were up and open. What had been a lifeline for many during and immediately after Hugo, blossomed into a forum of hope and reconstruction. A week after the storm, with power returned to the building, my own healing moment occurred in the production room after our Saturday shift. I wrote, composed and recorded "Chainsaw" in two hours that morning. Before Christmas, we had sold 2,000 cassettes of the song, the proceeds split between the Red Cross and our Penny Pitch Children's Charities.

But the one thing that crystallizes that time for me came two weeks after the storm. My wife was speaking to a friend of hers at school one day. The woman spoke of spending that morning, huddled with her two children in a downstairs bathroom—a flashlight and a transistor radio the only comfort in the darkness. Her husband was out of town. She listened as trees crashed around and into her house. The storm passed. "But," she said, "it was when I heard your husband's voice...that's when I knew it would be alright."

To serve in the public interest.

Thanks to Don Russell, Mary June Rose and Bob White for their help in remembering salient details.

Charlotte: A City That's a Cut Above the Rest

Originally published in the Charlotte Observer January 1, 2004

Wow! I have the first Community Columnist piece of the new year. Not to worry. I shall remain humble. I also drew the April 1st column.

So what tribulations should I write about to mark the beginning of a brand new year and announce my presence with authority? What hot topic can I employ to Socratically stir the municipal pot of discussion? City Council? The arena? Developers run amok?

How about "My barber retired"?

How does this merit taking up important column-inches on the op-ed page? You must understand that he was no ordinary barber. Loran Smith had been cutting my hair since I was in the fourth grade. He started giving me buzz cuts at the barbershop in the Park Road Shopping Center back when Charlotte basically stopped at Woodlawn and Park Road. (Mr. Smith has graced the pages of the Observer before, although not for tonsorial reasons. A feature on his climate-defying banana tree made the local section about a decade ago.)

For nearly forty years Loran saw my head through all it's manifestations: adolescent fuzz, bearded long-haired hippie freak locks and back to middle aged fuzz. Even during my college days in Boone, a long seven month exile in Brunswick, Georgia and two years in Raleigh, I'd come back to Charlotte... and Loran for a hair cut. So I am in a quandary. I need a hair cut. What am I going to do? Again you may ask, how does this rate editorial status? For me, it was the seed for a larger question.

What ties you to a city?

What is it that not just brings you to a particular burg, but makes you stay there?

Your job? Possibly. But employment today is so ephemeral, job seekers wheel and turn like so many migratory birds, looking not so much for the right city, but for the right paycheck.

Your family and friends? Used to be where you were born determined where you stayed. Planes, trains and automobiles changed that. Cell phones and the Internet have put Ma and Pa as close as speed dialing or a mouse click.

What ties you to a city? A church? A school system? A sports team? A barber?

You need to know that I'm a Charlotte native. There are quite a few of us out there. We don't make a lot of noise. We do laugh quietly to ourselves when we hear folks who have moved here and claim ten or fifteen years residency pronounce their longevity as Charlotteans reason to take them more seriously than people who have lived here only, say, five years. Please don't interpret this as a slap at these relative newcomers. I'm a staunch advocate of Southern Hospitality, ya'll. But that's a whole 'nother column.

A friend of mine who was a fervent proponent of astrology once explained my link to the Queen City. She said Charlotte was a very Scorpio city and since I was a Scorpio as well, the bond was forged; the primary Scorpio trait being loyalty. Once a Scorpio is your friend, he's a friend for life... unless you mess with him. After the recent elections some local politicians might be able to identify with that.

Whether it's Charlotte or Chicago, Newton or New York, Lincolnton or Las Vegas, for some people there is a connection that moors them to that city and it cannot be broken. Stretched, perhaps, but never severed. The benefits of most municipalities - schools, transportation, the arts, jobs - and the liabilities - traffic, crime, taxes - vary only in degree. All cities bask in the former and suffer in the latter. Where the balance between the two is the most comfortable, that is where you plant yourself. The tap root might be your job. But it is the branching, smaller tendrils - a minister you trust, a favorite pub, a barber - that anchor you to the soil of a community. And as the soil feeds the plant, the plant feeds the soil; what you give back strengthens the city and the connection. (And if you'll allow me one final horticultural metaphor: as a city grows it is helpful to remember that a certain amount of manure can be beneficial.)

What ties you to a city? Make your own list of things on both sides of the equation. If it balances, stay and grow. If it doesn't, send me a post card. Especially if you find a great barber.

What Should a Southerner Salute?

Originally published in the Charlotte Observer April 6, 2004

There are some arguments that are simply unwinnable. The question of the Confederate flag is one of them. Democratic presidential hopeful Howard Dean's run-in with the flag is the latest example.

Heritage or hate is the argument. Both proponents can give credible voice to their view. Apart from saluting forebears who fought and died, the allure of the Confederate flag as a symbol is understandable. For older supporters it could represent defiance of a Federal government run amok. For the younger, it's an easily procured image of rebellion against any and all authority.

Unfortunately for the Heritage side, no matter how true their facts and pure their motives, the perception of any flag of the Confederacy is too entrenched in images of slavery – along with the KKK, outlaw bikers and other mouth-breathing, knuckle-dragging bigots – to ever be wholly viable as a symbol of heritage. But this is America, Land of the Free and home of the Bill of Rights. It is imperative that those who wish to venerate their Confederate ancestors have the right to do so.

So we find our culture at an impasse. One faction wanting to remember what was good and valiant in their past and another also within their rights not to have that painful past brandished in their faces through a battle flag. What to do?

Compromise. Find a different symbol.

I've been trying to think of something or someone that would be, at the same time, symbolic of Southern pride yet palatable to those who see any recognition of the Confederacy an anathema. It is not an easy assignment. Several possibilities have made the list, but the one I keep coming back to is Robert E. Lee.

In its first four score and seven years, our nation was not so much a nation as it was a loose conglomeration of smaller nations. The first drafts of the Declaration of Independence were scattered with individual colonies' wish lists and demands – much like so many appropriations bills in Congress today. But the idea of State is Home is Nation was far stronger than it is today. Yes, we're proud of the Old North State but betting some barbecue on a football game pales in comparison. "With all my devotion to the Union and the feeling of loyalty and duty of an American citizen, I have not been able to make up my mind to raise my hand against my relatives, my children, my home," Lee wrote to his sister in 1861. "I have therefore resigned my commission in the Army, and save in defense of my native State, with the sincere hope that my poor services may never be needed, I hope I may never be called on to draw my sword." His humble devotion to Virginia is evident. His position on slavery is less well known. In another letter from December of 1856 Lee wrote, "There are few, I believe, in this enlightened age, who will not acknowledge that slavery as an institution is a moral and political evil." His view that slavery would eventually end through the Christian salvation of the slaves over several decades was naive at best. His objection to abolition was less pro-slavery than it was a Southern gentleman's pique at outsiders sticking their noses in his nation-state's business, regardless of the validity of that business.

Lee is held in high regard by historians as a model of post-war Confederates, a man who may have embodied defeat at Appomattox but lived his remaining years dedicated to education and healing the wounded nation; not a bad symbol to acknowledge one's heritage. So make a new banner for Confederate heritage; a field of green – no red or blue from former ensigns – with a likeness of Robert E. Lee on it and relegate the Confederate flag to historical re-enactments and museums. Perhaps that way, whether or not our great granddaddies fought along side ol' Stonewall, Southerners as a group won't be thought of as a bunch of mouth-breathing, knuckle-dragging bigots.

This is one man's idea. Think it'll catch on? Probably not. I can already visualize the vitriolic Letters to the Editor from both sides of the issue. But you have to start somewhere. Compromise, especially after an Appomattox, is hard work.

Broadcasting's Life Blood

Originally published in the Charlotte Observer February 4, 2004

I donated my first pint of blood in 1973, the same year I got involved with radio. They remain tied together.

My dad was the impetus for donating. He started as a Marine in World War Two. I was quietly impressed by each new lapel pin he received from the Red Cross as he completed the next gallon. My first donation occurred working a campus station promotion at Appalachian State University. Broadcasting is in my blood and vice versa. I'd like to see radio in this city... and this country reach the same conclusion.

I have become curmudgeonly in my view of the radio industry, locally and nationally. Of all the symptoms I see of its demise, the most glaring is the lack of community involvement. The FCC's licensing requirement that radio stations should "serve in the public interest" was hammered into me relentlessly as a student. It was a defining slogan for me as a broadcaster. But years of deregulation and political manipulation of the industry have all but negated that mantra. Public affairs programming on commercial stations is usually buried in the wee hours of the weekend, if aired at all. Public service, once an important part of a station's image - not to mention their license renewal process - is reduced to liner cards read once an hour. A natural disaster seems to be the only event that can force stations to deal with their communities.

Which brings me back to blood.

I'm proud to be a regular donor with the Red Cross. Workin' on my 44th gallon, I am. Starting in college as a whole blood donor, I'm now involved in platelet aphaeresis. Once a month I get a call from the blood center scheduler almost begging me to come in. And no wonder. Blood supplies regionally are running at around 16% with greater shortages in the much demanded

O positive and O negative. One can assume the national rate is comparable. With the continued presence of AIDS, hepatitis and now the strict limitations placed on foreign blood, the decreased availability of blood has reached even more dangerous levels.

I believe two things. First, in every community there are dozens of old donors who have slipped away and more importantly, hundreds potential acceptable new donors; in cities the size of Charlotte, perhaps thousands. Secondly, I still firmly believe radio can still be a powerful force to serve in the public interest. And here's what radio can do.

In Charlotte there were 18 commercial stations listed in the latest ratings. Add the two public stations that serve the area and have a substantial listening audience.

Coordinating with the Red Cross, each of these stations would take a week and promote donating blood. And I mean promote the hell out of it. Make it as important as the national talking heads or a fund drive. Give it the same intensity that you give the next playing of Britney, OutKast, Elvis or the Dixie Chicks. Support it with personal appearances by your air talent and sweeten the pot with giveaways for completed donations. You'd be amazed at what loyal listeners will do to get a station coffee cup or t-shirt. Make it a goal to get 20 donors during your week, half of them new recruits. Do this on a rotating basis for one year. That's two weeks per station with some of the bigger wattages taking three. Commit to it. Don't renege. Don't miss your week. Don't slack off.

Folks can donate whole blood every 8 weeks. Six times a year. If only half of the listeners who respond become regular donors that's over 3,000 more pints of desperately needed blood for the year. And it would come in at a rate where it won't have to be thrown out as after the overwhelming response to 9-11.

Imagine what a difference radio could make.

To its everlasting credit, my professional broadcast alma mater, WBT, teams with its sister stations yearly for blood drives, continuing a portion of the public service that was once a hallmark of a great station. Perhaps WBT could be the catalyst to get the other stations on the bandwagon. I'd be happy to support the effort any way I could.

And I'd do it as a public service. I've got enough coffee mugs and t-shirts.

City Council Reality Shows? Why Not?

Originally published in the Charlotte Observer August 5, 2004

It all comes down to money.

What is the determining factor in any local government decision? Money. Other than proclamations naming next Tuesday as City/County Frog Appreciation Day, your local governments' primary jobs are to raise money and manage money. Whether it's paving roads, building arenas, or deciding which middle school gets a new bulb for their overhead projector, your elected officials are responsible for the ebb and flow of the fiduciary tides.

Managing the money, relatively speaking, is the easy part. Council and Commission members can rest assured there will always be something on which to spend the budget and that that figure will always go up. The piper must be paid, as well as the power company, the banks holding the loans and those pesky government employees who want a pay raise (that doesn't equal a fraction of the increase in a gallon of gas, let alone the cost of insurance.)

The tricky part is raising the money. I offer Flynn's Famous Aphorism #31 - if your out-go exceeds your income, your upkeep will be your downfall. Yet, finding lucrative ways to fill city, county and school board coffers without alienating those vexing voters is getting harder and harder to do. Raising taxes, for some odd reason, isn't popular with the vox populi. It's time, then, for some thinking "outside the box" to bolster the bottom line of city/county government. I respectfully submit a few ideas:

- Underwriting. Get sponsors for the Council and Commission TV broadcasts. WFAE, WTVI and WDAV do it. "This portion of the re-zoning hearing to put a landfill next to an middle school is brought to you by Greedo Development."

- While we're on the subject of TV, why not make the annual retreats our governing bodies attend into reality shows. Imagine the ratings on Channel

16 of the episode of "Government Survivor" where Patrick Mummford refuses to eat a large, live insect and gets voted off the dais. Not to appear sexist, but it would be up to Vilma Leake or Molly Griffin to marry Joe Millionaire and perhaps stave off another school bond issue.

- Sports contests. As soon as the ice is down in the new arena, split the county commission into Democratic and Republican hockey teams. You'd pack 'em to the rafters with just the possibility Jim Puckett would get two minutes for high-sticking Parks Helms.

- Sell corporate naming rights to the Council Chamber. Some radicals would say this is redundant. But I, for one, would love to see the Bojangles' Chamber if only to hear Pat McCrory say, "we gotta-wanna-needa-getta-hava motion..."

- Bill for trees. Problems like the Speedway flap would disappear. Simply charge $100,000 for every tree you want to cut down. Turn your property into the Mojave if you want, but it'll cost you.

- Smart auto stickers. If you work in Charlotte-Mecklenburg, but your address is outside the county, each time you cross the city/county limit, your sticker's bar code is scanned and 50 cents is charged to your Visa or Mastercard. (Boy, am I gonna get nasty mail on this one.) Sorry, but I'm one of the shrinking number of people who believe if you use something, you ought to pay for it - or at least help pay for it. If I get a new toothbrush, I'm the only one who uses it and should foot the entire bill. I'll never drive on every road in the county, ride on every bus CATS has or see every show at the Blumenthal, but they're part of what makes it worth living in the Queen City and makes businesses want to locate here. So, I have no complaint about paying for part of their upkeep. Also, when I ante up, it gives me the right to gripe about irrational or just plain stupid government spending.

And the frosting on the cake of my money-making scheme - the annual City Council/County Commission Bake Sale. This should be a ginger snap, even if the rumor that Bill James and the Pillsbury® Doughboy were twins separated at birth is false. This is how it works, ladies and gentlemen. You sell enough cakes and pies and you can hold your annual retreat in Pinehurst. If not, you get the leftovers and a fresh pot of coffee in the multi-purpose room of one of our fine middle schools. I understand they just received a new bulb for the overhead projector.

Turn Me Loose on Traffic Scofflaws

Originally published in the Charlotte Observer March 5, 2004

Traffic in Charlotte is like the weather. Everybody grouses about it but nobody does anything. As a concerned Charlottean I am ready to take this heavy burden upon my shoulders.

What are the problems? I see two – scofflaws and money. Scofflaws are the speeders, the red-light runners, drivers who block crosswalks, etc. I call them Drivers Of Limited Thinking or DOLTs. The money side of the equation is reduced budgets for road construction and repair, police and mass transit.

Here's the solution.

Hire me. Give me a squad car, a radar gun and turn me loose on the DOLTs. It doesn't have to be a new cruiser, just one of the old Crown Vics that still runs, has working air conditioning and blue lights. I'll pay for my own gas and maintenance. (Hey, it'll be tax deductible.)

I'll go through whatever training is necessary to make my enforcing presence on the streets legal. I'll learn the traffic laws, how to write out a ticket and the psychology of not beating the bejeezus out of some DOLT who was doing 57 mph through a school zone. Since I'm approaching the age of AARP the physical fitness part will have to be modified to Police Training Lite, but then I won't be hotfooting it after bad guys down dark alleys, will I? This training will establish me as the first CMTM - Charlotte-Mecklenburg Traffic Monitor.

How does hiring me as a Traffic Monitor solve the problem? First, let's take a quick look at the traffic picture in Charlotte as represented by one road, Independence Boulevard. According to a 2001 24-hour mid-block count by the Charlotte Department of Transportation, Independence east of Albemarle Road is the busiest road in Charlotte, carrying 97,000 vehicles . . . and that count is three years old. For the sake of argument, let's say that 1% of those vehicles are exceeding the speed limit.

I'll pause for a moment while you control your laughter.

If I, as a CMTM, were to catch just 10% of that 1% in the course of a day, that's 97 speeding tickets. At $50 a pop, that's $4,850. I'll give the city 50% of that, a quarter goes to taxes and maintenance, leaving me with $1,212.50 for a good day's work.

One slight drawback – I'd never bag 97. If I could nab one speeder every 15 minutes, that's only 28 scofflaws a day, allowing for a lunch hour. The answer, of course, is more CMTMs. We wouldn't all have to work the major thoroughfares. We could be assigned to the roads around our neighborhoods. I volunteer to take Sardis Road from Randolph to Highway 51 (59,000 vehicles per day) and Rama up to Monroe (17,200 vpd). It wouldn't have to be full time, either; just a couple of hours each day to impress upon DOLTs that speeding is, after all, against the law. Part-time CMTMs would also reduce accusations of quotas. Just give me enough money to cover my expenses and the rest I chalk up to civic duty.

Recruitment wouldn't be a problem. All the city would have to do is ask for anyone who, while driving, had ever said, "Man, I sure wish I was a cop right now." And no, this wouldn't turn the Queen City into the Speed Trap City. Speed traps are abrupt changes in the lawful limit intended to snare tourists. CMTMs would merely enforce the well posted speed limits.

And the numbers? If 50 CMTMs each caught 10 speeders a day, it would produce $9.1 million over the course of a year. Add in red-light runners and the jackpot gets even bigger. I'm not sure how this windfall could be spent, but perhaps we could fix a pothole or two. Get the trolley up and running. Maybe give a pay raise to officers so they wouldn't have to moonlight managing parking lots at football games. CMTMs could take that over, too, as well as other mundane things like directing traffic when signals are down and give the real police more time to chase bank robbers . . . or have a home life.

So make me an official Charlotte-Mecklenburg Traffic Monitor. Put me on the road. Speed past me. Go ahead, DOLTs . . . make my day.

Crossing the Comedy Line

There are lines.

They are ubiquitous. From sports fields to traffic lanes, they show us direction, keep us safe, mark boundaries. They also delineate behavior. These last lines are becoming harder and harder to define, walked on and rubbed into obscurity like the chalk borders on a base path after nine innings.

The most recent and celebrated overstepping of these lines was by CBS News. I won't rehash that here. There have been enough pundits screaming "Off with their heads!" to last for a good while. I will bring to your attention another line-crosser, also on television, Mr. Bill Maher, and an episode you probably haven't heard about.

Mr. Maher is no stranger to controversy. Comments he made several years ago on his ABC program "Politically Incorrect" culminated in his exit from the building. For the most part, I've enjoyed Bill's humor. It's edgy, sometimes thoughtful, and skewers politicians, poseurs, and the self-inflated of all stripes with equality. But he is also among the growing number of comedians who are opting for the easy laugh; the cheap shot. Case in point:

On his September 25th broadcast of his HBO series, Mr. Maher chose to try and find humor in the death of James Cockman, the Sara Lee executive from South Carolina who was kidnapped and suffocated, on the day after his body was found.

His boorish witticisms took a personal toll. As he was uttering his insensitive jokes, my wife was on the phone consoling his niece, one of her good friends.

This may sound like a private beef to you. And, in a way, it is. Mr. Maher's crass comments hurt a friend of ours. But they went beyond that. They affected the community as well.

Comedy – and one of its sharper components, parody – have always tiptoed that fine line. Social commentary that also gets a laugh is hard to do. I consider well crafted humor in this vein a worthy and necessary endeavor. Lenny Bruce, George Carlin, and Richard Pryor lead the list of notables whose standup routines entertained, shocked, and promoted thought at the same time. Bill Maher has shown he has the same capabilities. His irreverence, and yes, even courage in asking tough questions and harpooning the pompous – regardless of race or creed – has been commendable. But his tasteless targeting of a good man's senseless death is something I can't recall from any previous comic of that caliber. In doing so, he not only lowers his own standards, but those of the audience he is trying to entertain. I don't know what troubled me more – his jokes or the fact that the audience laughed at them. I should say, some of the audience. There were more than a few questioning groans. After his second one-liner on the subject, Mr. Maher himself seemed slightly embarrassed. Perhaps he realized, albeit too late, that he had crossed the line.

It's difficult not come off sounding like some radical, espousing humor temperance. "Register hand guns and punch lines!" In my 25 years in professional media I have reveled in humor and parody, occasionally stepping up to that line that denotes propriety. To my knowledge, I've only stepped over it once, and made a public apology for it.

What it boils down to is responsibility. Those of us that command the attention of the public's eyes and ears have a responsibility to live up to the trust given to us. Whether that trust involves presenting the news, making people laugh or pushing the edge of the envelope while shaking up entrenched ideas, those in the media – especially at the level of Mr. Maher – need to remember this and be taken to task when they don't.

I'll end with the words of America's premier social and political humorist, Mr. Mark Twain. "Always acknowledge a fault. This will throw those in authority off their guard and give you an opportunity to commit more."

. . . and try to leave 'em laughing.

So, What's an Old Bus Station to You?

Originally published in the Charlotte Observer June 3, 2004

Those who cannot remember the past are doomed to repeat it.
-George Santayana-

History is more or less bunk. We don't want tradition. We want to live in the present and the only history that is worth a tinker's damn is the history we made today.
-Henry Ford-

So. Are George and Henry for saving the old bus station or against it?

To go to bat for saving anything, whether it be a statue, a building or a wilderness area, requires a passion fueled by personal feelings. Personally, I don't have them for the Trade Street Bus Station. In the nearly fifty years I've lived in Charlotte I may have visited it twice, neither a very memorable experience. I have fonder recollections of the old Douglas Municipal terminal; walking out to the gates under the walkway's corrugated metal roof, swirled in the combined hot wind of a Carolina summer and prop-wash as Eastern Airlines brought my dad home from a business trip.

But that's just me. Tens of thousands of other Charlotteans came and went through those bus station doors, Some faced the excitement of their first solo sojourn, some the weary boredom of another predictable junket. Mothers and fathers kissed their sons and daughters off to Grandma's or camp, college or war. Wives welcomed husbands, kids scanned countless Trailways windows for the first glimpse of that special someone. Sentimental claptrap? Perhaps. But maybe it's that sentimentality that keeps us in touch with our humanity in a world that grows seemingly more inhumane.

I think of the Charlotte landmarks that have meant something to me. When Richard Nixon visited Charlotte in October of 1971, I stood on the steps of the Masonic Temple on Tryon Street. The Myers Park High School Marching Band was the first band along the parade route. It was a heady experience. Norman Kaneklides, who was on the color guard, had his fake, white rifle taken away by the Secret Service. The President of the United States passed – very quickly – within 15 feet of me, a chubby sophomore baritone horn player, all while I stood on the steps of what many have called an architectural marvel. Neither my memories nor experts' opinions saved that building.

Last week I noticed the McDonald's on South Boulevard at Atherton was closed. No big deal. McDonald's are as ubiquitous as dandelions. But my first job was in that McDonald's. What great memories! 16 years old and flipping burgers and *making money*. Being hit by a quick change artist and finding out I'd taken *him* for $10. Seeing if my pickle slice would stick to the ceiling longer than Eric Hallman's. No big deal; they're building a new one two blocks down. (Which raises the question, why close a money-making business that employs quite a few folk while the new place is being built? I'll leave that to Doug Smith.) This building wasn't even the one I worked in. Same site, but my store had the huge Golden Arches; the Big Mac was still on the culinary drawing board. And yet, it hurts – just a little – to see one of the landmarks of my life consigned to oblivion.

You may have gathered by now that I'm a preservationist. Many of the younger and perhaps newer residents of our fair town are not. Possibly the reason they aren't interested in preservation is because we old guys, being such poor stewards, have left them nothing in which to be intrigued. I have no personal interest in saving the bus station other than a desire to turn ever so slightly from our path of all things – *all things* – being disposable. With the great economic minds that people this city, there should be a way to appease the passions of personal feelings while placating fiscal practicality. And while we're at it, instead of taking the millions sought for by the Arts community to build a new theater uptown, why not take that money and restore the Carolina Theater to its functional glory?

I have some pretty neat memories of that place, too.

Inside a Re-zoning Battle

Originally published in the Charlotte Observer July 7, 2004

A re-zoning battle is being waged in my neighborhood.

I have been hesitant to discuss it here. It felt wrong to use this community forum to air something that was basically a personal complaint, even though it concerned a process dictated by city rules. But a new wrinkle has been added to this particular re-zoning petition that could impact re-zoning decisions for the entire city.

Petition Number 2004-046 concerns nearly three acres on the corner of Sardis and Rama Roads. You may have seen the house and property – a heavily wooded lot graced by a large Victorian-style farmhouse. The Miller house, as it's known around here, dates back to the early 1900s. For the past several years it's been a private residence, also operated as a bed and breakfast. It was on the market for a while, but there were no takers, until John Tallent made an offer. Mr. Tallent is an undertaker and has proposed to buy the house and property and convert it into a funeral home. To do so would require re-zoning the property from residential (R-3) to office (O-1[CD]). Neighborhoods around and adjoining the property – mine among them – have protested the re-zoning.

When business concerns begin a re-zoning process, especially one that might not be too popular, they hire experts to help shepherd the petition through the tangled web of city bureaucracy. Walter Fields was brought in to work Petition 2004-046. Mr. Fields has great expertise in the area, having served on the city's planning board for many years. His knowledge of the ins and outs of re-zoning, along with a relationship and access to council members not available to the average citizen, make him an effective advocate for his clients. As a group, we neighbors are learning a few of those ins and outs, but we are nowhere nearly as schooled as Mr. Fields. He is also a very affable man who meets with sometimes hostile opponents, trying to get what his clients want, while ruffling as few neighborhood feathers as possible.

In fact, all parties concerned – the owners, Mr. Tallent, Mr. Fields and the neighbors – are good people, all are trying to look out for what they feel are their best interests. The owners should be able to sell and get on with their lives. Mr. Tallent is a competent, caring businessman. Mr. Fields is doing what he was hired to do. And the neighbors should be able to protest what they feel is an unsuitable re-zoning and have their government handle it fairly.

Here comes the wrinkle.

The city plan for this particular area of Charlotte allows for residential and institutional zoning. The first is evidenced by the hundreds of single family homes making up the neighborhoods. The second by the schools and churches surrounded by those neighborhoods. The closest businesses are miles away. Under current definitions, the city recognizes funeral homes as businesses, not institutions. For this reason, and citing parking and traffic among concerns, initial reports from the Zoning Board were unfavorable for the re-zoning.

Walter Fields wants to try and change that. By asking for multiple extensions on the decision by the Zoning Board, Mr. Fields basically wants to circumvent the process, causing delays that would allow a possible ruling to make funeral homes not businesses, but institutions. And not just the one proposed for the corner of Sardis and Rama, but new ones everywhere.

I don't mind a fair fight. I've dealt with Mr. Fields before on re-zoning in the area. And while the outcome wasn't totally satisfactory from my point of view, concessions were made within the constraints of the process, and a compromise was reached. But Mr. Fields' tactics in this petition are questionable. He doesn't like the way the decision appears to be going, so he's attempting to change the rules near the end of the game.

Well, boo-hoo, Mr. Flynn. Nobody said life is fair. The cry of NIMBY has fallen on deaf ears in City Hall before. A funeral home isn't exactly an asphalt plant. And goodness knows opposition by a majority hasn't stopped the Council from making up its own mind, for good or ill.

The families whose homes border the property, the homeowners in the other neighborhoods, and parents of children who attend Providence Day School across the street, await the decision of the Zoning Board and the City Council. I'm waiting to see, should the Board favor the neighborhoods, what other loopholes Mr. Fields has at his disposal. And you, fellow citizens, should watch what transpires in Petition 2004-046. As in all re-zoning petitions, what's going on in my backyard could very well affect yours.

Oprah's Web

Originally published in the Charlotte Observer 2007

I emailed Oprah last week.

The open forum on her web site to ask questions, voice concerns or offer programming ideas is laudable. There is a caveat posted, however, stating that, due to the vast amounts of correspondence Oprah receives, I probably wouldn't get a personal reply. In other words, I'll probably get more media attention speaking Farsi into my cell phone. Such is life.

I wrote Ms. Winfrey regarding her role in the live-action film version of *Charlotte's Web* due out at Christmas. The trailer for the film was part of a string of coming attractions drilled into my eyes and those of my eight year old, along with 40 or so other youngsters and parents, during a recent screening of the animated epic *Barnyard*. The feature lived up to the expectations of the younger audience, down to mine, but I was ready for that. I wasn't quite ready for the highlights of *Charlotte's Web*.

Charlotte's Web by E.B. White, recognized as one of the best-selling children's books of all time, has enjoyed – and in some cases, endured – several adaptations since its publication in 1952. Mr. White's other works – *Stuart Little* and *The Trumpet of the Swan* – enjoy the same popularity with children and adults alike. His opus chronicling the adventures of Wilbur and friends has won numerous awards. Along with his works for children, White wrote and edited for the *New Yorker* and other prestigious magazines. He updated William Strunk's *The Elements of Style*, the best known book on American English writing guidelines. For his decades of literary achievements, he was elected to the American Academy of Arts and Letters in 1973. He received a special Pulitzer in 1978.

The upcoming holiday release features some very big names; Julia Roberts voices the talented spider, Oprah appears as Gussy the goose. Reba McIntyre, Robert Redford, Cedric the Entertainer and Steve Buscemi help fill the cast. Initially, I had hopes this version would live up to the standards the cast – not to mention the author – typifies. Those hopes were dashed when one of the focal points of the trailer was Templeton, the rat, being knocked off a fence by a cow breaking wind.

Being a Boomer and having three kids, I've been around *Charlotte's Web* for a long time. I have always enjoyed the book. For children, Mr. White's book can impart important messages about relationships and responsibilities, not to mention early lessons on death and dying. In the author's words, it's "a story of friendship and salvation on a farm." Beyond that, *Charlotte's Web* is a fun read for everyone. Admittedly, it had been a while since I last trod the yard at Zuckerman's farm, so I went back to the book and searched it cover to cover. For the life of me, I can find no passage where Mr. White uses bovine flatulence for any reason, least of all a cheap laugh.

OK, poots can be funny. Especially for kids. Why are whoopie cushions such big sellers? Perhaps, I reasoned, my pique was just a symptom of the onset of Creeping Curmudgeon. But then, I've never found much humor in gratuitous gas-passing, with the exception of the campfire scene from Mel Brook's *Blazing Saddles*. (Yes, there is a vast difference between satirical farce and needless production of methane.)

But it's getting out of hand. Current conventional wisdom, especially that of the film's producing company – Nickelodeon – requires any film geared toward the younger set to include some sort of close encounter with a bodily function; the grosser, the better. It was this "dumbing down" of media, particularly for children, where my correspondence to Oprah found its origin.

Over the years, Ms. Winfrey has become an admirable champion of literacy. Her views on books and reading, and their ties to self-esteem, have been no small portion of her popularity and credibility. The scene in question seems to be the antithesis of those efforts.

Now, hold on, girlfriend . . . I'm not Oprah-bashing. I doubt that Ms. Winfrey had any idea the cow gas vs. rat scene was part of the script. (The web site for the film lists the director and a bevy of producers, but no writer. Embarrassment, possibly?) Most voice talent these days get their "sides", record their lines, then go on their merry way without seeing a complete script or, for that matter, the other actors. If I were Oprah and had been asked, along with Julia and Robert, to voice a character from one of the most respected and beloved children's books, I would have jumped at the chance, too.

Hopefully my email has alerted her to something she ought to know about and could possibly rectify. There aren't too many people in the world who could "suggest" a cut from a major motion picture, but I'd put a couple of bucks on Oprah. As I said in my email, "Editing out a scene like that would do no harm to the film. Leaving it in harms *Charlotte's Web* – and those associated with it – a great deal." The rest of this incarnation of Charlotte's Web may be wonderful. But because of that scene, and out of respect for Mr. White, my family and I will . . . um . . . pass.

Primaries, Deaths and DMV

Originally published in the Charlotte Observer September 2, 2004

Some random thoughts and idea starters:

As we wade ever deeper into the election season, I keep thinking back to the primaries. Your tax dollars and mine paid for them. Why should they? Aside from the fact that voter turnout for the primaries, from a percentage standpoint, is usually abysmal, primaries are not "elections", but "selections"; political parties selecting who they feel has the best shot at winning the election (or being the juiciest sacrificial lamb.) So, if primaries serve only the political parties, why shouldn't they pay for 'em? They can still use the facilities, but when the dust settles, the Board of Elections sends the bill to the RNC or DNC rather than you and me. Then, in the general election, when everybody – Democrats, Republicans, third and fourth party candidates – has a stake in the results, I'll be happy to pick up part of the tax tab. Perhaps to finance the primaries, the Donkeys and the Elephants could take some of the 527 money used to make attack ads that all politicos say they dislike and channel that cash into making the process a little more cost effective for the taxpayer. Make a negative into a positive. Wow, what a concept.

In October of last year, I made a note of a headline from this paper: "Female G.I. Dies in Bold Daylight Attack." I was troubled by it then and it still bothers me. Back then, I wondered why the differentiation was made based on gender. Was the death of a US soldier any more terrible because it was someone's daughter, rather than someone's son? In a society where one of our mantras is "save the women and children", probably so. I can't remember if this was the first young woman to die in Iraq. "Firsts" usually garner more ink. And that's what bothers me now. The "firsts" are long forgotten. The deaths of soldiers are no longer the news for 1A or the lead at six o'clock. As the body count grows, the media – and unfortunately, my own mind – seem to gloss over the "nows".

For another thought on Iraq, in particular on the recently released report on the goings-on at Abu Graib, I quote from Bill the Bard's Henry V; Act III, Scene VI, "... and we give express charge, that in our marches through the country, there be nothing compelled from the villages, nothing taken but paid for, none of the French upbraided or abused in disdainful language; for when lenity and cruelty play for a kingdom, the gentler gamester is the sooner winner." So much for learning from our past.

Finally, there are three letters that strike fear in hearts of everyone who owns or drives a car – DMV. Recent adventures in getting a car title transferred and qualifying a 15 year old to drive allowed me to observe the DMV processes first-hand. Telling myself I was observing kept me from screaming and hair-tearing. The title transfer alone took three trips with hour-long waits each time. I am conscientious. I went to the DMV web site. I read all the signs in the contract station on Independence (the signs are as numerous as the cars on Independence.) Yet each time there was some little nugget of required information absent from my carefully prepared package. The employees at DMV have one of the most thankless tasks in the world: explaining state auto bureaucracy. They explain it over and over, all day long, to people who don't read the signs, who often speak something other than English, who always have an excuse and usually don't have a clue about what they need. I offer an idea to grease these squeaky would-be wheelers. As many of the bigger banks do, the DMV should set up a Help Desk. Get rid of the gumball machines and have a desk – perhaps two – where, if you aren't sure if you have the correct documents, a friendly DMV Associate could show you the error of you ways before you spend an hour in line. That might speed things along once you get to the lady with the license plates ... unless there was a hour wait to get to the Help Desk. A word to the DMV Wise that you won't find on the web or on a sign - don't use White-Out on a title application.

Let's Skip the Flag Fashions

Originally published in the Charlotte Observer August 23, 2003

From Title 4 US Code, Chapter 1 Sec 8(d): *The flag should never be used as wearing apparel, bedding or drapery.* And from Section 8(I): *The flag should never be used for advertising purposes in any manner whatsoever.*

Obviously, the folks at Tommy Hilfiger haven't checked their office copy of the Flag Code recently. Otherwise they probably wouldn't have designed the women's panties using the Stars and Stripes that were advertised in last Sunday's Observer.

I've watched the proliferation of American flag products with dismay. The boom in displaying Old Glory after Sept. 11th was understandable, even laudable in all but some of its more jingoistic respects. "Rally 'round the flag" was never more truly demonstrated. After the initial fervor waned, there was still an ongoing current of patriotism during the actions in Afghanistan and then Iraq – if not supporting the policy, then supporting the men and women in harm's way. It's good to see the American spirit, embodied in the flag, displayed properly.

Properly.

Oh, great, you may be saying. Here come the flag police. Can't you just be happy that the flag is being exhibited? Can't you just let people show their patriotism in the way they see fit?

Nope. Sorry.

The U.S. flag is the symbol of our country and should be treated with the respect that engenders. It should be flown proudly and properly. It should be carried or displayed as prescribed in Section 7 of the Flag Code. For those of you who don't want to wade through the Code, the easy rules are that the flag is always the highest on the pole and placed on the right. And when the flag is too old or worn, it's destroyed, preferably by burning, with an appropriate ceremony. Simple.

I am not a flag-waver in the arrogant sense of the phrase. I don't espouse "my country right or wrong". My patriotism is rooted in my father's service in the Pacific during World War II. I do stand when the national anthem is played. I place my hand over my heart and recite the Pledge of Allegiance. I don't get all lathered up when protesters burn a U.S. flag. It is their right to do so and there are things this nation has done that deserve to be protested. There are a lot of protesters. There are a lot more flags.

But I do get upset when the merchandisers of America try to blatantly cash in on our national colors. Some examples:

The flag should not be on paper plates. Can't have the symbol of our country tossed in the trash with the leftover baked beans.

It should not be used as a logo for selling fashion T-shirts or bandanas. The emblem of 227 years of freedom shouldn't next year's dust rag.

The pursuit of happiness includes being comfortable. Does that mean you should plant your rump on an American flag-festooned promotional seat cushion? I think not.

And – shame on you, Tommy Hilfiger – the U.S. flag should not be material for ladies underpants. The "half-mast" jokes alone should be a deterrent.

I fully expect the stores – Belk's, Old Navy, Dillards, et al – now appropriately chastised, to remove the merchandise that profits from patriotism from their shelves and sin against the Flag Code no more. Yeah, right.

The Flag Code, while officially a law, is more a set of guidelines. Each state is allowed to set its own, though most tend to adopt the Code. Enforcement of 4 US Code (the Patriot Act notwithstanding) is lax. It's hard to rank sitting on a flag seat cushion up there with smuggling shoulder-fired missiles into the country.

But perhaps if you think about it, out of respect, a few of you will skip the flag T-shirt for some other fashion. Out of a small bit of national pride you'll buy the paper napkins with flowers instead of the flag. And for you all-American gals that want to show your love of country, I suggest you pass on the $15 flag panties and go get a flag kit. I found one on line that includes a flag, pole and bracket for $12.99. You save two dollars, you're just as patriotic . . . and more people will be able to see it.

What Color's My Grassroots?

Originally published in the Charlotte Observer May 30, 2007

I'm a leader.

It has been confirmed by the two major political parties of the United States of America.

I'm one of the "grassroots leaders" of the Republican Party. Tim Morgan, the new Treasurer of the Republican National Committee told me so in a letter dated. . . well, it says Monday morning, so even though I'm a leader, I'm not sure when it was mailed.

Howard Dean, Chair of the Democratic National Committee, sent me the 2007 Grassroots Survey of Democratic Leaders to fill out. He doesn't call me a "grassroots" leader but he does refer to me as "a Democratic leader" in my community and since I got a Grassroots Survey I feel the title can be assumed. There's no date on his letter, either, but there is a spiffy tabulation code on the survey.

The salutation on Tim's missive is simply "Dear Friend". Howard gets a little more personal. The "Dear Fellow Democrat" has been struck through with a blue line and replaced with what appears to be Dr. Dean's hand-written "James". The blue line even slants slightly upward with a kind of personal flair that surely no computer could imitate.

Tim is fulfilling a promise he made to RNC Chairman Mike Duncan that he would contact me immediately to get me "back on our team" and renew my membership. Be assured, Mike, Tim has made good on his promise. He contacted me. It will be hard, however, to get me "back" on the team as, to the best of my recollection, I've never been "on" the team. I could be mistaken. As anyone testifying before a Congressional committee can tell you, recollections are tricky things.

Howard wants me to help the DNC "tackle tough issues" and help "fix the mess created by George W. Bush and his Republican cronies." He wants me to become a member of the DNC. I appreciate this magnanimous offer. It's probably not often someone who has been a registered Republican for 34 years is offered a chance to be a Democratic leader, grassroots or otherwise.

The "cronies" reference seemed a bit strong, but I've seen Howard on You-Tube and he can be emotional at times. Tim doesn't partake in name-calling per se, but does mention his desire for "stopping the Democrat power grab."

Both letters offer a carrot/stick approach to win my membership. On the carrot side Tim offers a "bold agenda" of lower taxes, new jobs and homeland security, while Howard has cheaper prescriptions and better education. Hooray for both!

Tim's stick is Nancy Pelosi "pushing our country to the extreme left." Howard says "the American people have had it with President Bush" and those darn cronies of his in Congress.

Both letters are asking for money. I'll wait a moment while you recover from the shock. Both the RNC and the DNC are willing to accept my personal check. Luckily, in the American spirit of instant accessibility to proffered funds, both Committees happily take Visa, Mastercard, American Express and Discover.

Donation to the DNC - $25. Donation to the RNC - $25. Supporting the Party of my choice and earning frequent flier miles or getting cash back? Priceless.

Howard states my opinions (and money) will build the Democratic Party into a force that "can win anywhere, including the reddest of red states." Come on, Howard...

Tim implies that the RNC has no special interests to "bankroll" their campaigns "unlike the Democrats". C'mon, Tim ...

So. Who to join? To use another credit card motto, "membership has its privileges." What color are my grassroots? Should I send my green to the red guys or the blue guys?

The problem is I'm kind of purple; conservative on some issues and liberal on others. Neither one of the two major political parties seem to be speaking to me, at least not in these fund-raising letters.

Thanks, Tim and Howard, but I'll pass on membership for now. I will return your survey, Howard. Someone may actually read it. In the meantime, I will continue to vote, as is my right and my responsibility, for the more qualified candidate, regardless of his or her party.

It's probably too much to hope that this kind of partisan panhandling will diminish. But here's a tip, Tim and Howard. It might help to send me a fundraising letter – and a candidate – that, instead of relying on the pronouns "us" and "them", uses the pronoun that begins our Constitution – "we".

Support Live Theater

Originally published in the Charlotte Observer May 6, 2004

"Every artist was first an amateur."
Ralph Waldo Emerson - Progress of Culture, 1876

Mr. Emerson must have had a precognitive moment concerning Charlotte area theater. We have a bunch of amateurs in this town.

Please do not take the word "amateur" in a pejorative sense. The dictionary says an amateur is someone who engages in the arts, sports or sciences as a hobby rather than a vocation; that is, folks that do something for the love of it. The majority of the theater community in the Charlotte region fit this description. They act, direct or do tech because they love it. I fit snugly in this category, whether as a question of pay or talent depends on which critic you read.

How many people are involved? MTA, the Metrolina Theater Association, lists 67 performing arts groups in the region. That's a lot of actors. Of those, only 14 are listed as "professional" companies with Charlotte Repertory Theater the only Equity group. (Actors Equity is the professional actors' and stage managers' union.) The other 53 are community, college and high school theaters. And while the other professional theaters outside of Rep pay their actors, it is nowhere near what would be called a "living" wage. A running gag in theater circles asks, what's the best way to improve the aerodynamics of an actor's car? You remove the pizza delivery sign. Some actors are paid as little as $50 for six weeks of work. Again, this isn't a complaint. Many would trod the boards for free, but they'd rather make it a viable career. Is it any different anywhere else in the country? Go to New York or L.A. and see how many waitresses, sales clerks and gas station attendants are really actors. And while actors are no more guaranteed a job in their chosen profession than brick masons or CPAs, the job pool is somewhat shallower.

Back to our local scene. The two things all these companies have in common are a desire to put on a good show . . . and they charge admission.

Now to heart of the matter: a recent column in one of the theater publications asked the question, what can be done to make area theater better, more vibrant and more profitable? I have several suggestions.

Vibrancy, I feel, is not an issue. The range of dramatic offerings in our area is incredibly wide. Small companies like Bare Bones, Actors Theater and C.A.S.T. are constantly pushing the envelope. There are numerous playwrights groups who do staged readings, hold workshops and support the craft. From edgy shows to the chestnuts, there is usually something for every theater taste in production all year.

"Better" is reasonably subjective. Theater tends to be Darwinian. If the show is incomprehensible, the actors are bad, the direction is worse and the sets look like wet cardboard – or the Board of Directors is comprised of idiots – odds are that company won't last long. Practice makes perfect or at least better. Time will improve the quality of theater here.

More profitable is a trickier question. First, the smaller theater groups shouldn't count on local government for help. Money does come from that quarter occasionally, usually belligerently, so don't expect it. The Arts and Science Council's pie has only so many slices. Fill out the forms correctly and you may get served. The bottom line for theater profits is more bottoms in the seats. How do you get them?

You get them by advertising. Budget more of your small and precious bankroll for it. (More importantly, groups like ASC and MTA should start an ongoing advertising campaign to educate the community on the joy and excitement of live theater.)

You get them by supporting other companies. As theater folk, you owe it to your fellow artists to go to their shows.

You get them – and this is going to hurt – by lowering your ticket prices. Yeah, the road show of Le Miz is getting $24 a head for the cheap seats. And yes, you have royalty concerns, too. But be realistic. Hitting the cineplex is only $7. Would you rather have 10 people per performance at $15 each or 50 at $5? Many companies have Pay What You Can nights. Have more.

That's what theater types can do. You, the Kind Non-Thespian Reader, should spend one night a month pried away from the house and see what these crazy, talented, passionate amateurs are giving to the cultural life blood of their communities.

Will you like every thing you see? No. But how many nights have you said that about the 78 cable channels you pay for?

Bumps in the Election Road

Originally published in the Charlotte Observer November 5, 2004

> *"Half of the American people have never read a newspaper. Half never voted for President. One hopes it is the same half."*
> *-Gore Vidal-*

It was 6:30 PM on Election Day. I'd just gotten home from work. My wife and I stood in front of the television watching the early returns. I remember being scared, thinking, "This cowboy is going to get us into World War Three," and proceeded to watch them count the votes in Ronald Reagan's landslide victory. No, it wasn't the day before yesterday. It was 1980, just three days after our wedding.

As I write this on Halloween Eve, there have been five presidential elections since then; a sixth under our collective electoral belts as the ink on this page dries. World War III has yet to occur (though some may argue that point) and my heartfelt trepidation of 24 years ago has subsided a good bit. (Newlyweds are inherently nervous.) The inference, then, is that I have become blasé about the political process. This could not be further from the truth. I view our elections to be the vital core of our identity as a country, even with the predicted phalanx of lawyers from both political wings ready to challenge, delay and confound the outcome. With all its warts, this is the design for choosing our leaders. No nation in history had done it exactly this way before we did.

Did you think the process had been running smoothly until Bush-Gore four years ago? Not so, fellow voters. There have been bumps in the road from the beginning.

The first presidential election was won, of course, by the first George W. Basically, Washington ran unopposed. Political parties weren't a factor until the election of 1800, so back in 1789 there were no running mates; the person who got the second-most electoral votes – John Adams – became the vice-president. (Two small political tidbits – North Carolina cast no electoral votes in 1789. The state hadn't ratified the Constitution yet. And Clinton from New York got three electoral votes. Not Hillary – another George.) Two hundred years ago, Thomas Jefferson won the election with 162 electoral votes to Charles Pinkney's 14. There is no record of the popular vote – the first records of what the people thought didn't come until 1824 – but I would wager there were stuffed ballot boxes and 19th century equivalents of hanging chads.

There have been electoral dust-ups in quite a few presidential contests. The one in 1800 resulted in the Twelfth Amendment. Elections in 1824 and 1836 were so convoluted, they'd flip your Whig. I'll leave it to the individual to dig into them. And one of the bugaboos of the 2000 election had nothing to do with Florida, but with Texas. The Twelfth Amendment says an elector cannot vote for Presidential and Vice Presidential candidates who both inhabit the same state as the elector. Dick Cheney was living in Texas and was registered to vote there, but moved back to Wyoming a few months before the election. The suit challenging the electoral allotment due to his residency was dismissed by the Northern District of Texas Court.

Granted, up until the 2000 election, any dispute in electoral voting was handled in the House of Representatives. The involvement of the courts may have muddied the waters for a few years, but I feel sure America can weather these Constitutional storms.

From Andrew Johnson's impeachment and Harding's Teapot Dome to Nixon's Watergate, Reagan's Iran-Contra and Clinton's impeachment, we have seen the best and worst of our leaders. In each of these historic tests of our country's political mettle there have been many who predicted the downfall of the government. In each instance we've come roaring back a little sadder, perhaps a little angrier, but a great deal wiser.

I envy you, fellow voters. As you read this, you have the luxury of knowing, at least at first blush, the results of our great national privilege. Stuck back here in the past, I can only wonder at what will transpire in the voting booths of America and look forward, with a tad of 20th Century trepidation, to the excitement of the days to come.

I do regret, just slightly, being two days late in wielding the immense power I hold as a Community Columnist to bend the will of undecided voters, as some of my colleagues were able to do. To the winners, congratulations. To the losers, wait 'til 2008. To those who didn't vote, don't complain.

My Tenure as Community Columnist

Originally published in the Charlotte Observer December 2, 2004

My final Community column. So much to say. So little time and space.

I considered recapping the year and let you know how folks responded to my musings. Some responses, like a few of the ones regarding my idea for changing the flag used to salute Confederate heritage, are unprintable. Most of them were thoughtful, intelligent and complimentary, even when taking an opposing side. Therefore, take heart, readers. Not everyone is imbued with the narrow-minded vitriol that pops up in Letters and the Buzz – and even in other local columns. Thank goodness, though, they are allowed their ink, if nothing more than to remind and warn us of what dark corners remain in this world.

I've always felt that this forum, so graciously opened to me, should be used to focus on this community and how it relates to the larger community of the nation and the world. It should get you thinking and talking. It should shine a little light into those dark corners when possible. So, rather than rehash old issues, let me leave you with a few fresh seeds to sow in the New Year.

O.K., I lied. One partial rehash. For those of you facing re-zoning petitions, don't give up the fight just because some of the big ones have been lost. Continue to learn about the process and get involved. Make *illigitimi non carborundum* your credo. Now, to the new stuff.

I met Mark Mathis only once. He seemed like a nice guy and talented beyond his on-air antics. Whether you feel his dismissal was justified or not, getting canned in broadcasting is the nature of the beast; more so now than ever. John Boy Isley once told me, "There are two types of stations. The ones you've been fired from and the ones you're about to be fired from." Don't worry about Mark. When he gets healthy, and if he stays that way, there will be plenty of opportunities for him, on or off the air.

Speaking of career changes, there is a little known, forty year-old trade agreement concerning textile quotas that's getting ready to expire after the first of the year. Experts say it will allow China to corner possibly 90% of the world's textile market. It will be interesting to see the reaction when cities all over the world, including those in the European Union start feeling like Kannapolis.

I look forward to the day that advertising agencies get off the bandwagon of using ugly little dogs to promote their products. It was cute – briefly – after *Men in Black II*. That was two years ago. Move on.

As big a fan as I am about the idea of light rail, I starting to feel our city's foray into this form of transportation might become a mini-version of Boston's Big Dig. It will be finished, but late, over cost . . . and it'll leak. (On a transportation side-note, I've always wondered why some city has never contacted the Disney Corp. and studied their monorail system. Seems to be a fairly reliable conveyance. And talk about sexy and identifiable . . . perhaps it only works in magic kingdoms.)

This holiday season, give yourself a break from the world. Don't run away from it. Just leave Iraq, Rather, recounts, light rail, Dubya and Condi, T.O. and the towel, Artest and the beer cup on the back burner for a few hours. Trust me, they'll continue to simmer there just fine. Take those two or three hours to do something that has little or no hype involved in it. That includes skipping the latest Hollywood blockbuster and turning off the TiVo. Enjoy one of the local theater holiday shows. Take in the Helga exhibit at the Mint. (One of my aspirations in life is to own a Wyeth.) Read a book that wasn't written by a former member of any presidential administration. Or – if you'll allow me a shameless, self-serving plug in my last Community column – find out what First Footin' at Rural Hill Farm in North Mecklenburg is all about. Then jump back into the world. Somebody needs to keep an eye on it. It might as well be you.

Thanks. And adieu.

Backword

By Doug Robarchek

When James K. Flynn, the World's Largest Leprechaun, asked me to write a backword to this book, I quickly agreed. But I had one tiny question: What the hell is a backword? I looked up "foreword" in my Shorter Oxford English Dictionary, and it said, "A preface." So I looked up "preface," and it said, "The introduction to a literary work, stating its subject, purpose, plan, etc." So what's a backword? An afterword. A postface. The farewell to a literary work. Which raises the question: Can the writings of James K. Flynn be considered a "literary work?"

For years, James K. (never Jim or Jimmy or Jimbo or anything else) has mined the rich vein of humor that lies beneath Charlotte like the Reid lode. He has explored it, assayed it and sprinkled the landscape with bits of mirth tossed off like so much refuse. Sort of litter-ary work. But if you examine those observations that he has thrown around so casually, you find that many of them are, in fact, golden little nuggets of silliness and, sometimes, serious satire.

Yeah, his stuff is literary, all right. Where it fails the dictionary definition is in the word "work." James K.'s stuff never reads like work, no matter how much skull sweat he may put into it. It's always like play. Whimsical wordplay.

If a foreword is an introduction, an afterword is a bye-bye to some literary byplay. Sort of a byeword. This one starts with a nod to a bygone Charlotte:

When I came to town in 1980, with my dear friend and favorite former relative, Peg Robarchek, Don Russell and James K. Flynn were a major part of WBT's endearing stable of likeable, charming personalities, along with Henry Boggan, Rockin' Ray Gooding, H.A. Thompson and others. In those faraway days, Charlotte radio in general and Russell and Flynn in particular were a class act. They were witty and genuinely funny, and they didn't insult the audience's intelligence.

One day back in the early '80s, Peg told me Russell and Flynn had used the word "callipygian" on their show.

I said, "'callipygian?' It sounds like a squab from the west coast."

She said, "that's what they said, more or less."

OK, maybe I liked 'em because their jokes were as dumb as mine. But I also liked them because they would use a word like "callipygian." Oh, look it up, for cats sake. Do I have to do all the work around here?

In fact, Russell and Flynn impressed Peg enough that the hero in her 1992 romance novel "Tallahassee Lassie" was a radio jock she named "Russ Flynn." Here's how she described Russ Flynn when the heroine got her first look at him, in the swimming pool:

> "He was tanned and sleek all over -- hard calves and well-toned thighs, slim hips beneath the water-drenched swimsuit, a belly hard and flat and bisected by a downward swirl of wet curls, a muscular chest."

Wow. If you've never seen James K. Flynn, let me tell you, that's an uncanny description of the man. Of course, if you have seen him, you know I'm lying. James K. is built more like a futon.

But he's a smart and funny man. A Renaissance Man of entertainment. An expert radio personality, advertising writer and voice. A terrific columnist. A poet, who has served as the self-appointed "Poet Lariat" of an off-and-on beer-and-verse group we both belong to, the Brew Pub Poets Society. The public-address announcer for the NBA Charlotte Hornets. And a fine actor, who has appeared in numerous theater productions. Not so long ago I saw him in the title role of "I'm Not Rappaport." As he always does and always has, he made me laugh.

He also can write with grace and style. Discussing what ties a person to a city, what determines "where you plant yourself," he writes, "The tap root might be your job. But it is the branching, smaller tendrils -- a minister you trust, a favorite pub, a barber -- that anchor you to the soil of a community. And as the soil feeds the plant, the plant feeds the soil; what you give back strengthens the city and the connection. (And if you'll allow me one final horticultural metaphor: As a city grows it is helpful to remember that a certain amount of manure can be beneficial.)"

Ladies and gentlemen, James K. supplies that manure.

So OK, I like the guy. Still, you may be wondering what I am doing here in the back of his book. I know I am.

You may be asking the obvious questions: What is this guy Robarchek trying to say here anyway? Who is he anyway? Why should I care anyway? Why is this thing called a "backword" anyway? Who did put the "ram" in the rama-lama-ding-dong anyway? Why does he say "anyway" all the time anyway?

Well, you certainly are full of questions, you little magpie. And I wish you luck in getting some answers, because I sure as hell don't have any. Especially about why James K. wanted a "backword." Is it because he's a little backward himself? Is it so he could put it in the back of the book instead of the front, to avoid alienating readers right at the start? Or is it because he just has to turn the familiar, the accepted, the usual, on its head?

That last one is my personal theory. James K. is as playful and full of mischief as an otter.

On the radio he created regular characters like the coach of the Bush League (during the presidency of George I); the Rev. Anklebone of the First Lucre Apostolic Sweet Haven Church, or FlashChurch; local bluesman Nearsighted Muddy Catawba, and Egyptian farmer Jim-Bob Farouk. Russell says, "One of my favorite memories of James K. is how he could literally develop a character on the spot. Before the arrival of the Ramses exhibit at the Mint Museum, (longtime newscaster) Bill Walker was doing a series of stories from Egypt. WSOC-TV had a daily spot on the air teasing what Bill would be covering that night. One day, the copy read something like, 'Join Bill as he explores the ancient ways of farming that are still maintained by some people.'

"I said something like, 'Egyptian farmers? What do you farm in a freakin' desert, for crying out loud?' Well, that's all it took, and James K. invented this character Jim-Bob Farouk, and we ran with it for over two years." Russell recalls James K's description of the typical ancient Egyptian farmhouse: "They always kept a small sphinx near the cook-stove. If the family moved, they'd take everything but the kitchen sphinx."

OK, OK, nobody hits a home run every time. But for a very long time, at least since the days of Jim-Bob Farouk and his mummy, James K. Flynn has been making Charlotte chuckle, groan, laugh out loud, and even think.

So I still don't know what "afterwords" are supposed to be. But if they are the words we leave that live after us, James K. doesn't need me. He has written his own.